Hez

Chronicles of a Mighty Man

Hez

Chronicles of a Mighty Man

Jonathan Cope

Chapter illustrations by
Amelia Howarth

The Christadelphian
404 Shaftmoor Lane, Hall Green, Birmingham B28 8SZ, UK

2020

First published 2020

ISBN 978 0 85189 431 7 (print edition)
ISBN 978 0 85189 432 4 (electronic edition)

Printed and bound in the UK by
CMP (UK) Limited

Contents

Prologue

THIS BOOK attempts to imagine the life of one of David's mighty men. The man in question is called Hezrai the Carmelite. He is mentioned in 2 Samuel 23:35. Apart from his name and home town, and the fact that he was a mighty warrior who was loyal to David, we know nothing about him whatsoever. But if we had a record of his life it would surely be a fascinating read.

- How did he become associated with David?
- What was it like for him both before and after David's ascension to the throne?
- How did he respond to the king's sin with Bathsheba, the death of Uriah, and Absalom's rebellion?
- What about events in Jerusalem once the uprising had been crushed?

In all of these matters, and more, I have tried to paint a picture of everyday life in Israel, without adding anything that might be detrimental to the Biblical narrative. I hope that what I have suggested in the following chapters reflects, at least in part, what life might have been like for those who knew David and remained true to him.

What we do know is that this time period abounds with fascinating incidents. With faithful words. With promises and prophecies. With acts of greed, violence and stupidity ... but also of courage, love and faith. The lessons leap from the pages of scripture for us.

In David's day, a number of great men remained loyal to him, acknowledging him as the king of Israel, chosen by Almighty God. True believers today also know that one day, the rightful king will return and take his place on David's throne. Like those in days gone by, they wait in faith for God's chosen one to come and reign.

Jonathan Cope
Coventry, April 2020

Chapter 1

The sorrow of an orphaned child

MY MEMORIES of that horrendous day in Carmel are very clear. I may have been just nine years old, but it seems like only yesterday. The sky was slate grey, mirroring the proceedings perfectly. I can still hear the elder's words, still see the pitying looks of the men of my city, and the stunned faces of the children. I can still hear the sobbing of the women. And I remember the cold. A bitter, biting, wind swept in from the Mediterranean, bringing with it a fine spray from the sea, and the kind of icy cold that gradually eats into you, numbing every part. But I already felt numb. No freezing blast from the Great Sea could have made me feel any more traumatized than I did already.

My Dad had died when I was only two years old. He was known as Hezrai (or "Hez", for short). As his only son, I was given the same name. I have absolutely no recollection of him whatsoever, mainly because, even in those formative years, he was hardly ever at home. He was a soldier in the army of King Saul, Israel's first mortal king. Those who knew him told me he was a superb warrior. His bravery was legendary. "As fine a swordsman as I ever saw" was a phrase which I heard more than once from those who had served with him.

One day, in the fields outside Gaza, he found himself separated from the rest of his battalion and surrounded by Philistines, baying for the blood of their Israelite invaders. One of his closest friends, who had been with him through many similar skirmishes, was there as well. He was a short distance away but unable to reach him to offer assistance. He saw my Dad take out four of the enemy in that final conflict, before a Philistine arrow pierced his heart. His comrades were able to retrieve his body, but by then he was already dead. He was laid to rest in Carmel.

Saul wasn't present at his funeral. His son, Jonathan, attended in his place. I am told that he spoke of my Dad's faith and valour. He described a man who put others first, a man who served Israel's God with great determination and with no thought for his own safety. Little did any of his family and friends know how soon it would be before others would be laid alongside him.

My Mum was a fantastic woman: kind, patient, loving and funny. Strict over things that truly mattered but never making a fuss over trivialities. I heard others call her "a marvellous mother in Israel"; it was a great description of her!

At the end of each day she would sit down with me and recount one of the incidents from the history of our nation. I learned about Abel, Enoch, Noah, Abraham,

Isaac and Jacob. I heard of Joseph, Moses and the Exodus. She would tell me about Joshua and how our people had taken the land of Canaan under him. My favourite story was the one about the sun standing still in the sky, enabling Joshua and the people of Israel to defeat their enemies. She would also teach me about the Judges: Ehud, Deborah, Barak, Gideon and Samson. What a mixed bag they were!

And, of course, there was Samuel. This great seer was still alive during my early years. His presence in the land was truly wonderful; like having an angel of God amongst us. When I was seven years old, we went to hear him speak in Bethel. Although I was too young to comprehend much of what was said, I still remember being amazed by the way he delivered his message to the multitudes who had gathered to hear him. He had such authority – such presence. It was clear that he was a man of God. Those from Carmel who had travelled to listen to him walked home in silence, awestruck by what they had heard.

So, even without my Dad around, those early days were happy and fulfilled. There wasn't much money to spare, but we didn't want for anything. At least, not until that terrible winter, when that dreaded fever swept through the villages and towns of the south, and its icy fingers touched every member of our family. Every member, except one.

My two sisters died within a day of each other. Both had been crying out, moaning for days on end. One moment hot and sweating, the next freezing cold. An incessant, hacking cough that seemed to tear them apart, gradually getting worse by the day. Their bodies were laid in the family tomb. Within a week my Mum was with them. She had been unwell for weeks but, typically, had never complained. When she wouldn't wake up that last morning, I ran round to the neighbour's house, pleading for help. But there was nothing they could do; nothing anyone could do.

And so, as I stood by the tomb of my family on that terrible day – all alone in the world – the numbness caused by the weather was in keeping with the sorrow, uncertainty and pain that racked my mind. I watched as the large stone was rolled to the mouth of the cave, and heard the final words of the elder who oversaw the day's proceedings. They are seared into my memory:

> ***"And so, as we commit the body of our dear sister to the ground, we look to the day of resurrection, when the promised seed will come ..."***

As I dwelled on those words in the years that followed, I wished I could have found comfort in this. I may have done at the time; it's all a blur to me now.

For an orphan in Israel, it was customary for a family member to step in. My grandparents had died before I was born, and my Mum was an only child. Although Dad was the youngest of a large family, most of his brothers and sisters lived in other parts of the land. Two of his sisters even lived in Moab. So that left just one man: my Dad's brother, Uncle Jed, who kept a vineyard a mile or so outside of our city. The little I knew of him was not particularly positive. I know that he and my Dad didn't see eye to eye, and we had very little contact with him during my childhood. Even now, as I recall the day of my Mum's funeral, I can still see that vile, hypocritical look in his eyes. When he knew that everyone was watching him, he proclaimed that he would do the honourable thing and take me under his wing.

"This dear child will be like the son I never had", he assured his audience, reaching out and placing a consoling arm round my shoulders. The others who were there looked on with what was, I thought, a degree of scepticism.

Yes, my uncle's eyes were full of kindness and benevolence ... until we were alone. Then that generosity turned to apathy or, more correctly, to outright hatred. I know he never wanted me around.

Maybe he and his wife, Aunty Jemima, didn't like children. Perhaps they objected to having to share the little that they had with me. Maybe they were just selfish. Although I was never abused, I certainly wasn't loved. The bedtime stories about men and women of faith became nothing more than a distant memory. I can't recall either of them hugging me, teaching me, or encouraging me in any way. They wanted me out of their sight as much as possible. And that led, unerringly, to trouble.

It wasn't that I deliberately set out to be naughty. Initially, I wanted to be respectful. To honour my new "parents" as I had honoured my Mum. But trying to honour people who are so dishonourable is very hard; for a child, it's virtually impossible. After a while, I simply stopped trying.

By the age of twelve I was virtually wild. I'd go missing for days on end. I never attended school; never listened to the readings from the law or went to the synagogue. I became part of a gang. There were three other lads, all of them older than me, and all in a similar position. Javan and Tiras were brothers – orphans from the neighbouring town of Maon. Jabez, like me, was from Carmel. His Mum was still alive, but she didn't care what he did or where he went.

We lived off the land, coming home only when we felt like it. We would hide out in caves, taking refuge from the storms which buffeted the countryside, transforming the green fields, cloaking the vineyards and olive groves in a garment of mist. We would steal and lie. We began by letting animals out of their enclosures, chasing them through the fields. We moved on to breaking down walls and burning trees and haystacks. We got into fights with those from other villages and towns, and came home bruised and bloodied. We revelled in our status as rebels.

I knew that my uncle was being told to rein me in; that he had to discipline me. But he had his own demons. Uncle Jed was a drinker. A pitiful, pathetic excuse of a man who spent most of his nights with his one true love – the wineskins – and most of his days sleeping it off.

By the time I was fourteen I was as tall as my uncle and far, far stronger. He tried to punish me ... but only once. He had been cornered by three men from the city – elders, who sought to uphold the law and guide those who were going astray. I know exactly what they told him. I was lying on the flat roof of the house that evening and heard every word they said:

We revelled in our status as rebels

"Time to take him in hand, Jed ... before it's too late ... this is what Moses' law demands of you ... you have a duty to act ... he'll thank you, one day."

When he saw me, he took off his belt, ready to teach me a lesson.

"Hez", he said sternly, "this is something I should have done a long time ago."

The resulting struggle was totally one-sided – almost comical. It ended with my Uncle flat on his back, nursing his bruised ribs, whining like some wounded animal, his great, bloated, purple face a picture of suffering. I could have hurt him more than I did, had I wanted to. I didn't do so. Not out of gratitude for the minimal amount of care he had shown me, more out of pity.

In a final act of defiance, I wrestled the belt from his grasp, pinned him to the ground and glared into his terrified, bloodshot eyes. I felt the coarse leather between my fingers, knowing that I could very easily have used it on him as he had intended to do to me. No words were spoken, but we both knew exactly what I was thinking: that I had ultimate power over him, and there was nothing whatsoever that he could do about it. I stormed out of the house, knocking over chairs and the flimsy table as I went, leaving my uncle on the floor, gasping for breath like a whale beached on the shore at Joppa. I then took that belt and threw it down the well in his neglected vineyard. That was the last time he ever dared to raise a hand to me.

Aunty Jemima was a timid little mouse of a woman, terrified of her own shadow or of doing anything that might upset her drunken lout of a husband. Towards the end, she hardly spoke to me at all.

Of course, I was heading for disaster. Maybe I just didn't care. Life had been so good until my Mum had died. After that nothing mattered to me. Nothing made any sense. It was as though everything that was truly important to me had been snatched away in an instant. So, if I hurt others or was hurt myself – well, what did it matter? No pain could ever be as bad as the agony which I felt at being all alone in the world. Perhaps I wanted others to suffer like me. Deep down, I think I had concluded that this would be somehow "fair". Then everyone else would know what it was like for me.

I never spoke to anyone about my feelings: the agony that tormented me, day after day, the terrible pain, like a dagger through my heart, that wouldn't go away. It was there when I fell asleep, and it hit me as soon as I woke up. No – I never said a word. I bottled it all up. And like wine fermenting in one of Uncle Jed's wineskins, it would have to be released one day. Little did I know how or when that would happen or what the consequences would be for me, or those around me.

Looking back, I can see the hand of Israel's mighty God at work in my life. At the time I refused even to accept His existence. While others spoke of the ten commandments, the offerings or the feasts, the covenants made in Eden, with Noah or Abraham – I shrugged my shoulders and walked away. How could I believe in a God who had allowed everything that I loved and cherished to be taken from me? But, just when I needed Him the most, He reached out to me in a most surprising and unexpected way. And only afterwards was I able to appreciate this.

The elders used to call this "providence". I never really knew what they meant, nor did I care. But now I do. The Almighty God of Israel was to provide something for me to fill that huge, gaping hole which had been left when my Mum had died. I needed a family. I needed a purpose. Both would be granted to me when one man took me into his care. He would feed me. He would teach me. He would forgive me. And he would love me. Who was that man? David, the son of Jesse, of Bethlehem. Without question, the greatest man I have ever known.

Chapter 2

Leaving home

BY THE time I was sixteen years old I had decided to leave Carmel for good. There was nothing to keep me there. There were certainly no family ties to bind me to the place of my birth. I had no cousins living locally, and Uncle Jed was all the encouragement I needed to spread my wings and seek a new life somewhere else.

On my last day under his roof I had exploded with rage at one of his comments. Normally I ignored him, but that day he definitely went too far. He was sitting, rather unsteadily, by the door, an old wineskin in his hand. He looked up at me from reddened eyes, his face a picture of loathing,

"Where were you last week anyway, Hezrai?" His words were slightly slurred, and he swayed a little, reaching out to steady himself. "Out with your little friends in the hills again? You live like an animal and you have the manners of an animal." He gazed at me with a look of total disdain, and then smiled. "Just like your Daddy", he added.

It was that last comment which touched a nerve. I didn't remember my Dad, but I would never hear a word spoken against him. I leapt to my feet and screamed at him,

"How dare you even mention my Dad! Perhaps if I'd been given more guidance I wouldn't be like this. Your problem is you only love one thing – wine. Nothing else matters to you, Jedidiah. Weak, weak, weak!"

I had no intention of hitting him, but he clearly wasn't willing to take the chance. I remember him scampering out of the door like some two-day old lamb caught in a thunderstorm, looking back over his shoulder, petrified in case I was following close on his heels. I last saw him peering round some ancient, barren vine at the side of the broken-down winepress, waiting for me to leave.

Aunty Jemima cowered in the corner of the room. I suppose I felt sorry for her, really. Although I had persuaded myself that I didn't really care, even I could see that having a drunken husband was no fun for her. She never had any spare money for luxuries, sometimes not enough even for the basics. On many occasions I saw her gleaning from morning till evening, scrabbling around the corners of fields for the scraps of wheat or barley, or picking the half-rotten remnants left on the fruit trees, desperately trying to gather enough for us to live on. She never knew whether the man she shared her life with would be lucid and reasonable, or (as was so often the case) unable even to stand up, let alone string a few words together.

I wanted to express my sympathy for this poor, terrified woman, but when I reached out to touch her shoulder, to commiserate – to apologise for my own actions – she whimpered and flinched, afraid that I might take out my frustrations on her. That's something I had determined never to do. No matter what they put me through, I would never hurt her physically. I may well have been wild and angry with the world, ready to do battle with anyone and everyone, but I would never hit her.

I remember gazing out of the window, seeing the sun beginning to rise over the fields to the east of the city walls. What a beautiful place Carmel was! In my early years I couldn't have wished to have lived in a better location. Mum used to call it "God's fruitful field". It wasn't until later that I realised why. Apart from the fact that it was, indeed, a fertile place, Carmel means "fruitful". I only had to look at the fields which were farmed properly to see how appropriate the name was.

Nabal was the biggest landowner in the area, so different from the rest of us. His fields stretched for miles to the south of the city. Great flocks of sheep and goats grazed contentedly everywhere. Solid, stone-built folds at regular intervals. Well-watered meadows. Vines, fig and olive trees, all with their succulent loads. Field upon golden field of waving wheat or barley. Massive barns, full to the brim with enough grain to tide him and his family over many a winter. What a tragedy that such great tracts of land belonged to someone like him! Even his servants knew what a fool he was. I often heard them

I remember gazing out of the window, seeing the sun beginning to rise over the fields to the east of the city walls

laughing at him behind his back. No respect at all. Just contempt. Utter contempt.

As a child, I remember hearing of others packing up and moving to the coast to work on the fishing boats or in the bigger cities and I could never see why.

"Better opportunities"; "the chance to make some ***real*** money"; "no more just getting by".

These were the kinds of things I had heard from those who departed. I thought they were mad. But that was until I had been deprived of everything that was important to me. With my parents and sisters in the family tomb, I had no reason to stay any longer. I wanted out.

I went over to the corner of the main room and drew aside the tattered curtain. This had been my "bedroom" for the last seven years. The old animal skins which had served as a bed from the day I arrived were still there. I gazed down at my few basic belongings. Then I reached up and retrieved the leather pouch from its hiding place. I suspected that Uncle Jed had gone through my things on many occasions in his desperation to "feed his habit". Had he found my money, he would have been down to the local inn within seconds – so I always made sure it was safely tucked away, and I had changed the hiding place regularly. I felt the few coins inside the pouch. I had virtually nothing. Even if Uncle Jed had been inclined to give me anything – what could a man like that give? He'd trade anything for his next cup of cheap red. Oh, how I wished he could have been more of a father to me, to comfort me, to guide me, to be a friend when I needed one. But it could never be.

I gathered up my few clothes, my hunting knife, bow and arrows and, most importantly – my pride and joy – the goat's hair tent, and made for the door. Living in the outdoors can be hard, even in Israel. Sure, the summers are normally warm and long, but when the rain sweeps in, everyone takes cover. Some days during the winter can be bitterly cold. I'd never seen snow, but I'd heard that they had it in the north, in places near to the border with Lebanon or Syria. I'd known wells – occasionally even streams and waterfalls – to freeze over. A decent tent is the only hope for someone living as a traveller in such a land.

I had worked in Nabal's fields for the entire summer the year before, trying to earn enough money to buy myself a few simple belongings. But how would I ever be able to afford a tent, especially one which wouldn't fall to pieces in the first few weeks? It was then that I received what I believed to be an incredible slice of good fortune. Nabal's wife, Abigail, was often out in the fields with the workers. Truly she was an amazing woman: hard working, caring and stunningly beautiful. Despite her wealth, she always wanted to know how the servants were. Many times I saw her give food or items of clothing to those working on the land – but only when her husband was away.

I was astonished when, one day, she stopped and asked me how I was and if I had enough to eat. She seemed to be genuinely interested in my well-being. She told me to help myself to some of the grain and take some more home for Aunty Jemima. It was the first time any adult had spoken to me in such a way for many years. I explained that I wanted to buy a tent to be able to travel. I said I was saving everything I received from my stint in the fields, and told her why. Towards the end of the summer, when Nabal was visiting family in Gilead, she came to see me. She said she had come across something that might be of interest to me.

"It's only an old tent, Hez", she explained, "but I wondered if you might be interested in buying it? We don't really have any use for it here, so you're welcome to it."

When she showed it to me, I could hardly believe my eyes. It wasn't old. In fact, it was obviously virtually new – the goat's hair was barely bleached by the sun, and it was in excellent condition. A decent size. All the poles and ropes were intact. And the price: just five shekels – it was too good to be true! I did the deal there and then, congratulating myself at what a shrewd businessman I had become.

Now when I was young we had a phrase we used about others who were a bit "slow". We would say that the one in question was "not the swiftest arrow in the quiver". It really wasn't the kindest thing to say, but it was something I had heard (and said) very often during my early years. Well that was certainly true of me that day! Only afterwards did I come to see that Abigail had been very generous to me. She knew I needed help. She had probably paid twenty or thirty times as much for that tent – but when Nabal wasn't around, she let me have it cheap. What a wonderful woman she was.

I checked the leather straps which bound the tent together and heaved it effortlessly onto my back. Unsurprisingly, there was hardly any food in the house for me to take. I had determined to pick some fruit or buy something on the way. Once again, I gazed down at Aunty Jemima, still motionless on the floor, obviously waiting for me to leave. And this time I felt a genuine pang of sympathy for her. What a miserable life she had! At least I could escape to the hills and valleys of Judah. She was trapped with Uncle Jed, twenty-four seven. I reached into the pouch and took out four shekels – half of all I had left after buying the tent, knife and a few other essentials. Slowly, I walked over to where she was, still crouching silently in the corner of the room. I knelt down beside her.

"Aunty Jem", I said quietly, "I'm sorry for all the trouble I've caused you. Here: this is for you."

I laid the four coins on the floor by her side.

"Don't let him get his hands on them. Buy something for yourself for a change. You deserve it."

At first, she didn't stir. But then she looked down at the money, then up at me. For what was, I think, the first time in my memory, I saw her smile. The transformation was astonishing. I saw in those deep brown eyes the love and care of a woman who had wanted to do more for me for all those years, but had been trapped by her animal of a husband.

For a while she didn't say anything. Her lips moved but nothing came out. It was as if she was struggling to find the right words. Eventually she spoke:

"Bless you, child." Her voice was quiet and full of emotion. "Bless you. Keep safe. And please, don't blame the Almighty for what has happened to you. He cares for us all. I know He cares for you. Trust in Him. Pray to Him. Our Father's glorious wings are outstretched over His children. He will bless you. You will achieve great things in His name, Hez. I know it. I just know it."

In a final act of kindness and unity, she reached out and clutched my hand. I was, I must admit, a little taken aback by her words – and even more so by the strength of her grip. After about twenty seconds, she pulled my hand towards her and kissed it, just once. She then released her hold and, without another word, gathered the coins from the floor.

I turned and made my way out of the house. I didn't know where I would go – maybe north to Hebron first of all. It seemed there was always building work going on there. Then perhaps up to Joppa, where I'd heard that there were boats that needed building or repairing. I had no desire to go to sea, but if the money was good ... who knows? Possibly even up to Damascus. I did wonder about enlisting as a soldier. But what about those reports we'd heard of King Saul? Who would want to serve in an army led by a man who had such violent mood swings?

As I reached the outskirts of the city, I turned and looked back. Carmel had been a very fruitful field for me ... at least for a while. But those hard days which had followed had transformed me from a carefree, loving, happy boy to a teenager with more than just a tent on his back. I was carrying a massive burden, and it weighed me down. The anger and frustration at what had happened to me remained, burning in my heart, despite those words of encouragement from Aunty Jemima. It would be some time before I would find the strength to let these things go, and move on.

A short distance outside the city I stopped and looked up. I had seen this monument so many times. I had read the inscription over and over again, thinking about my Dad and how he had served the man whose name this testament bore. I read it once more:

> ***"The words of Saul, son of Kish, the great and mighty King of Israel. The Amalekites are vanquished. The king's enemies are slain. His kingdom is secured forever."***

Even I knew that this contained, at the very least, some half-truths. We had all heard the story of how some of the Amalekites – including Agag the king – had been spared. We knew that this was contrary to the instructions of Samuel. We also knew that Saul had been told how abhorrent his actions were, and how angry he was with the seer for this. But could it really be true? Had he actually torn Samuel's cloak in a fit of rage?

Of course, by then the monument had already been erected, proclaiming the greatness of the monarch ... and there it stood, in my home town. By now, a little like Saul's kingdom, it was beginning to look rather tired. The mortar was starting to crumble. It was overgrown with weeds. The inscription was fading. I wondered what would happen to Saul and his royal house. Would Jonathan reign after him? Would another king arise to take his place? That's what some people were saying. But who would it be?

I turned and walked away, not knowing if I would ever return. For now, all that mattered was that I was heading out, away from Uncle Jed's house, to make my own way in the world. I hoped for fame and fortune. I dreamed of owning a massive house with servants, animals and fields. Little did I know that God had something very different – something far, far better – in store for me. But there would be times of hardship and danger which I would have to face first, on the journey of life.

Chapter 3

Big city life

WHEN IT came to it, leaving Carmel, despite its painful memories, was harder than I thought it would be. Sure, I had travelled far and wide before. I had been to Maon, and Kerioth in the south. On one occasion, with the other three members of the "gang", I had even reached as far as Engedi, on the shores of the sea of the Arabah in the east. It took us four whole days to get there, and even longer to get back. Those cliffs leading down to the shoreline were something else. But what a place! Little wonder it was also called the "Salt Sea" or "Dead Sea". Nothing could live in there. The high salt content meant that we could, quite literally, float on the water. It was unlike anything I'd ever experienced before. There were a couple of cities nearby. One was Nibshan; the other one, unsurprisingly, was known as "the City of Salt".

We had also journeyed west to the outskirts of the neighbouring town of Debir. That was one of our crazier adventures! We got into a massive fight just outside the city. It all started when someone accused me of stealing some figs and, before we knew what was happening, we had a full-scale riot on our hands. There were about a dozen lads, all intent on defending their territory – on upholding local pride. Despite being totally outnumbered, we came away with our heads held high. I can still remember seeing that miserable rabble scurrying back to the safety of their city, carrying a couple of their number who were out cold. We had out-thought and out-fought them. I think it was that day that gave me a feeling of invincibility. From then on I feared nothing and nobody. All the same, that journey away from the place of my birth, leaving the small amount of comfort and security I had enjoyed in the home of my uncle, was a momentous occasion for me. I knew it had to be. But I was still uncertain as to what the future might hold.

The first night, I camped out. It was a beautiful, still, clear night – surprisingly warm, so much so that I lay outside for the first few hours. A cloudless sky with a stunning blanket of stars filled the expanse of heaven above me. I lay there, amazed by the sight. I'd gazed at the stars many times before, but that night they seemed different, somehow. I know it sounds crazy, but those twinkling fires appeared to be speaking to me. I had some vague recollection of being told that they represented something else. The word "seed" came to my mind, but I didn't know why. Something to do with Abraham, perhaps? That was all lost to me now. It was so many years since I had heard anyone read those passages or explain them to me, and I had no interest anyway. Too much pain. Too many shattered dreams.

After three days I arrived at the suburbs of Hebron. On the way I had managed to work for a hill farmer who had paid me in kind – food and drink and a night's shelter. I could have stayed on, but I felt I had to keep moving as far away from Carmel as possible. Nothing, however, had prepared me for Hebron – or the challenges and dangers I would face there.

Hebron is one of the oldest cities in the land of Israel. Historians say it dates back over a thousand years – prior even to Abraham's day. They say he stopped there and built an altar to Yahweh when he first entered the land. Locals never missed an opportunity to tell "outsiders" about Hebron's rich past. To them, a place like Carmel was nothing.

The city itself was certainly impressive – bustling marketplaces, with an amazing supply of local (and some not so local) produce. Lots of fish, all sorts of cheese, eggs, sheep and goat's milk, nuts, honey, various different kinds of birds, clothes, leather goods and pottery were all for sale. Noisy taverns. Brightly painted houses, most of them three or even four storeys high. Some built as part of the city walls. I'd never seen so many people in one place in all my life!

The city abounded in ancient tradition and stories. As well as the account of Abraham and the altar, the tomb where he and various other family members were said to have been laid to rest was still there. The locals had painted it white. It looked more like a house than a tomb, with the surrounding area immaculately kept.

I had only been there for a few seconds when an elderly man cornered me, claiming to be one of Caleb's descendants. He took great delight in informing me – about five times in as many minutes – that Caleb was the man who had been granted the city when the land was taken under Joshua. He stood very close to me and delivered every word at a deafeningly loud volume. He went into great detail, describing how his ancestor had defeated the giants who had lived there previously, and had captured the city. That's when it was renamed "Hebron", or "seat of association". I think he expected me to be impressed by his family tree. I wasn't. I found it boring. I didn't tell him this, but I have to admit it did cross my mind. Thankfully, there was some sort of commotion at one of the market stalls and I was able to escape before he launched forth into another tedious tale of his forebear's heroic exploits.

It was a priestly city, and another local told me it was also a city of refuge. Again, while others would probably have acknowledged such facts with reverential awe, I just didn't care. All I wanted was somewhere to stay, eat – and a job. Incredibly, I found all of these on my very first day.

As I walked down one of the side streets, I found myself standing outside a busy carpenter's workshop. Four men were hard at work. Great beams lay in piles. Various items of furniture were stacked against the far wall. The sound of sawing and hammering filled the air; sawdust was everywhere. In the corner, one man was sitting at an old desk. He wasn't working as the others were; he seemed to be in charge. When he saw me, he called me over. He appeared far older than the others. His snow-white hair and bushy beard made him look ancient, but I suppose he could have been anything from fifty to eighty.

"New lad, eh? What do they call you then?"

"Hezrai", I answered. "But normally it's Hez."

He smiled as he spoke to me. His voice was kind and gentle. Unlike the others I had met, he didn't want to tell me how great Hebron was over and over again, or of his great-grandad's extraordinary ability as a giant slayer. He appeared to be genuinely interested in me.

"Where are you from then, Hez?"

"Carmel", I said, "I've just arrived today."

"Ah yes, the fruitful field. I remember visiting the city as a lad. Lovely place. Decent people as well."

Initially he appeared to be lost in thought, and I wondered if he had forgotten that I was there. He gazed out of the small window at the side of the workshop and again that warm, comforting smile spread over his face. Then he turned back to me. He asked politely what I was doing in the city, and I explained that I had decided to leave home, and was looking for work and somewhere to stay.

"Left home?" He seemed amazed. "How old are you, son?"

"Sixteen. I'll be seventeen next month."

"And you've left Carmel and come to Hebron ... with nothing but the clothes on your back and a few odds and ends?"

I nodded. He smiled at me once more – but it wasn't a smile of pity or disapproval. Strangely, he seemed to be impressed. I explained that my parents had died. I didn't go into detail but told him that I couldn't live in my uncle's house any longer. I decided to get to the point: I wanted work, and somewhere to spend the night. I didn't want to waste time chatting to some pleasant old man when I could have been out there, trying to find a room.

"Well, we're always looking for help here. As you can see, we're rushed off our feet. Have you done much carpentry?" he asked.

"Bits and pieces. I worked on the land last year and there were always tools and ploughs that needed mending. I did my share."

"I'm sure you did, my lad. I'm sure you did."

Once again, that generous, reassuring smile. What came next took me completely by surprise. He offered me a job and a place to stay. Two of the carpenters lodged with him and his wife, he told me. They had their own rooms and two meals a day. He said that the work would be unrelenting; if I was after an easy life, this wouldn't be for me. Much of their time was spent felling trees, then making beams, doors, window frames and other items to support Hebron's booming building trade. Apart from that it was domestic work: making and repairing chairs, tables and furniture mostly – and the occasional plough. The money was good, and if they had a decent month, there would be a bonus. The men who worked for him were all locals and, he told me, "a decent bunch". I was delighted; this was all I could have asked for! I accepted his offer, there and then. He seemed visibly pleased.

He stood up from his desk, and I saw for the first time what a great man he was. Slightly taller than me but with immense, broad shoulders and massive biceps. When he welcomed me to the firm by hugging me it was a bit like being hugged by a mountain bear! He took me round the workshop and introduced me to the other men. They were all friendly and polite, wishing me well. A bit of good-natured teasing about my having come from Carmel and my "country ways", but I wasn't at all offended. If anything, I was pleased; it made me feel like one of the team. At the end of the guided tour he turned to me and again that smile was there.

"My name's Aram. The lads call me Boss. There's not much of the working day left, so get yourself over to our place and settle in. If you explain to my wife about having met me, she'll make you welcome. Her name's Hanniah; most people call her Han."

As I walked to the lodging house that afternoon I felt ten feet tall. The "inn" as the locals referred to it, was large and basic, but spotlessly clean. Han was lovely. She had a kind, welcoming smile, exactly like her husband. She showed me to my room. It had a simple bed, a rail for hanging clothes, a basin and a large jug. It wasn't spacious but the view from the small, west-facing window was amazing – the city in the foreground, and then, in the distance, the hill country of Judah, stretching far away towards Lachish and the Great Sea.

Over the next few weeks things settled down and I soon got used to the routine of life in Hebron. Han's food was fantastic – tasty and lots of it. We'd start every day with bread, fruit, goat's milk and sometimes eggs or cheese. The evening meal was fish or meat (partridge or pigeon, usually), often in some kind of a stew. There were lots of vegetables: lentils, normally, and more of her beautiful freshly baked bread. Occasionally there were almonds to snack on, and sometimes even some honey. It was better than anything I'd eaten since my Mum had died.

The Boss was tough but fair. If anyone was slacking he'd be down on them. But when one of the men had a problem at home – his baby daughter was ill, I think – he gave him the next two days off and he and Han even called at his house to see how she was, taking some food in a basket.

For the first few weeks I ached from head to toe. My hands were red-raw from the work, and my back and shoulders felt as if I had been trampled on by a large herd of cattle from Bashan. I had always regarded myself as physically fit, but it was clear that the other members of the team were far fitter and stronger than me. Early one morning, the Boss saw me nursing my aching neck.

"Don't you fret, Hez. Keep stretching those muscles and you'll soon be fine."

He was, of course, absolutely right. Within a couple of months I was felling trees, cutting the wood into planks, making doors and frames and repairing items of furniture and old tools brought in by the locals. The aches and pains had gone. I was given some olive oil to moisten my hands, and they soon toughened up.

The other men liked to go drinking in the evening. I went with them every so often, just to be sociable, but soon made my excuses and left. I had seen what a lifetime at the wineskins can do for a man, and was determined that would never happen to me. I was more than happy with my own company, and I wanted to save everything I earned. After I had bought a few extra clothes, I put all my spare money in a wooden box under the floorboards of my room. In a short time I had saved more than I could ever have dreamed of possessing. A few months before I had wandered into Hebron with a few coins in my pocket and a tent on my back. Now I was rich – or certainly richer than I ever thought I would be!

One evening I was working late with the Boss. We were finishing off a chest of drawers for one of the locals. It was being collected early the next morning, and we had said we would have it ready. He promised to pay me more for staying behind, but I wasn't really that bothered. I knew he was fair and would reward me one way or another. It was the first time I had had the opportunity to chat with him alone since I had arrived. He asked how I liked Hebron, and working in the carpenter's shop. I told him I enjoyed the work, I adored Han's cooking and yes, I loved the city – so much life – so much variety.

"Well, Hebron is a special city", he said, pausing to wipe the sweat from his brow. "But there's a place further north that's far more important."

I was a bit taken aback. All I'd heard from the locals since the day I had arrived was what made Hebron great. According to most of them, it seemed to be the centre of

Within a couple of months I was felling trees, cutting the wood into planks, making doors and frames and repairing items of furniture ...

the universe. I was sure that some Hebronites had never been further than the city walls.

"What other place?" I asked, intrigued.

"Jebus", he said. "Or, at least, that's what it's called now. Still ruled by Gentiles, you see. Cursed Jebusites." His eyes narrowed, and then his face broke into his special smile.

"But you just wait, lad – in a few years that city will be ours again. Its true name is Salem, or Jerusalem. Others call it Zion, or Ariel. It will be the capital of this great nation one day. And" ... he paused for a few seconds and then lowered his voice ... "there'll be a new king."

I was astounded. A new capital city and a new king? I knew him well enough to know he wasn't the kind of man to make things up. I had to know more.

"How do you know this, Boss?" I asked.

"Well, that would take too long for me to explain, Hez. But youngsters like you should be prepared for that time and ready for the rightful king when he comes. King Saul's men don't take kindly to talk of another man having the throne, and I would hate you to get into trouble because of something I've told you. So, I'll tell you his name, as long as you keep it to yourself for the time being."

I assured him I would respect his confidence and waited for him to go on. After about twenty seconds, he fixed his gaze intently on me and simply said,

"David."

Around three months later I was given a couple of days off, and I took my tent out into the hills. It was the first time I had been truly alone since I had arrived in the city, and I was stunned by the beauty of the scenery, the abundance of wildlife, the peace and quiet, the feeling of being at one with nature. City life was exciting – but it was here, out in the wilds, where I felt most at home. I had decided that I would stay in Hebron for another year or so. I would save everything I earned and then head up to the north of the land – or maybe to the coast. If I had enough put by, I could even lease a little carpenter's shop somewhere and have men working for me. Then I would be set up for life.

Things finally seemed to be falling into place for me. I had it all planned out. Little did I know, but everything in my world was about to change – partly through the wickedness that lurks in the hearts of certain men, and partly due to my own stupidity and greed. That feeling of supreme self-confidence would depart and be replaced by fear and helplessness, the like of which I had never known in my life before. And it all began one day in Hebron's marketplace when I met a man from the tribe of Dan called Ben Obal, from the valley of Sorek. Nothing in my life would ever be the same again.

Chapter 4

A wolf in sheep's clothing

I HAD been in Hebron for about six months when the autumn storms blew in. They seemed to come upon us so very quickly. One week we were working outdoors with just our tunics on; the next we were wrapped up, with numb fingers and toes, shivering against the winds that screamed in from the coast. Working outdoors suddenly lost a great deal of its charm! The inn and the workshop were warm and dry, however, and there were far worse jobs. My workmates were friendly and encouraging, and Aram was as good a boss as anyone could have wished for. I promised myself that, when I had my own business with loads of men working for me, I would do everything in my power to be exactly like him. As I thought of what kind of master I could have ended up with, I breathed a huge sigh of relief that I had, apparently by accident, stumbled upon one of Israel's true gentlemen. Others were so very different.

The potter, for example, who had the shop and kiln at the corner of our street. I heard him screaming at his men almost every day, ranting and raging at the world over petty trivialities. And if someone dropped one of his precious pots ... well, the whole district knew about it. I once saw him pick up a young lad and fling him across the shop in anger. He reminded me of Nabal, back in Carmel. Nothing was ever right. All Nabal wanted was to be richer than everyone else around him. Never happy unless he was making someone else miserable. And if anyone dared to smile or laugh when he was in one of his moods, there was trouble. What a pitiful existence – for him, and for those closest to him. How did someone like Abigail bear it?

One Friday, work was slow, and Aram had given me and two of the other men the afternoon off.

"Just this once, though", he said with his customary smile. "I don't want you lot to get a taste for working half days."

In the marketplace, I stopped at a make-shift stall set up at the end of one of the rows, where a man in a bright blue robe was playing some sort of game. He stood behind the stall, and three lads – probably in their early to mid-teens – were in front. After a few seconds there was an explosion of noise. The man behind the counter roared with laughter and the three lads were left shaking their heads in exasperation, cursing at him. It appeared to be good-natured, though. As I didn't have much else to do, I wandered over and watched.

It was an old game; one of the oldest of all. The man had three cups and had placed a coin under one of them. He would then switch them round, and the audience had to tell which cup the coin was beneath. It was so boring that I nearly walked on. I had played this game with my sisters, all those years before in Carmel. But something made me stop. I think it was the fact that the man in charge seemed to win every single time. I couldn't work out why the three youngsters didn't give up. Maybe he was so quick that they just couldn't work out which cup was the one; perhaps they were desperate to win back what they had lost. I stood and watched, and I was sure I could follow the cup with the coin. Yes, there was no question about it – surely they could see it was the middle one? They placed their "bets" – all choosing one of the cups at either end – and he had their money again. Cue more raucous laughter and frustrated swearing. The man looked up at me:

"Ah, here we have a man of the world", he exclaimed, and the three teenagers seemed impressed. They gazed up at me with a look of respect. Strange, really, as I was only a few years or so older than they were. But I liked the idea that I was regarded in this way.

The man looked at me and smiled.

"Now, sir, how would you like to try your luck? There are very few in this great land of ours who are clever enough to catch out Ben Obal."

The three lads stood back, not quite sure what to say. Then one of them spoke up:

"You haven't got a chance, sir. He's far too quick."

I've always loved a challenge, and, anyway, it was only a few coins. What could possibly go wrong? As before, he went to work. The cups were switched round and straight away I knew I was on to a winner. I chose the right one and the man, with perfectly good grace, paid up. This pattern continued for the next three rounds. I won every time. The lads gasped in amazement.

"How does he do it?" I heard one of them say.

Next, I was challenged to hide the coin, and the man had to choose the right cup. I won eight times out of ten. He was left shaking his head in disbelief.

"He's so sharp. I've never seen old Ben beaten", commented another one of the youngsters.

After about fifteen minutes I decided I had had enough. I gathered up my winnings and started to move away. The man in the blue robe caught me by the sleeve.

"Sir", he said with the utmost sincerity, "I want you to know that you are special. Nobody's ever beaten me as many times as you have today. Well done!"

It was then that he hugged me. I must admit I was a little taken aback. I'm not sure that if I had just lost some money to a stranger in a market, I would have wanted to hug him. Nonetheless, I submitted to the embrace. Afterwards, he invited me to join him for a glass of wine. I declined. Again, he was fulsome in his praise,

"A wise man indeed. A man who is a drinker will never be rich. And neither will his family."

He spoke with such authority – such certainty and wisdom – that it was hard not to be impressed. We stood and chatted for a while. He was the very picture of civility. He told me that he was originally from the valley of Sorek in the area of Dan, but had come to Hebron to care for his elderly uncle. He was a tanner, and he explained that he had left his tannery in the hands of his two sons. Strange, but he didn't look like a manual labourer – they were normally stocky and with stained, rough hands. He was tall and thin, and his hands were spotlessly clean.

"Listen", he said to me as I was about to head home, "we're having a game this evening. A few locals. Only a bit of fun. You would be very welcome to join us. Maybe make a bit of extra money – you know, just in case the carpentry business dries up?"

I wasn't sure. Why get involved with gambling – especially when I was saving every shekel, hoping to move on and set up in business by myself? Maybe he read my thoughts because he drew me closer to him, apparently to impart some great pearls of wisdom. He spoke quietly, with immense feeling,

"Sir, a man like you – one as quick and clever as you are – will be sure to win."

Well, it seemed like a golden opportunity. Why not make a bit extra? I worked hard enough for Aram and, although the money was good, I would never be a rich man while I was employed by someone else.

The man told me where to meet him and hugged me once again.

On the way home the crowds were enormous. As I neared the inn there was a real crush, and I saw an elderly lady fall to the ground. Instinctively, I ran to help her, but someone tripped me up. I ended up in the gutter with my cloak smeared with dirt from the road. There were people all round me, pushing at me, while I tried to help her up. She thanked me about five times and wanted to give me some money to express her gratitude. I explained that this wasn't necessary – but as I walked away, I was suddenly aware that something was wrong. My money had gone! While I was on the floor, with all those people crowding round me, someone must have stolen my leather pouch. I still had the few coins in my pocket that I had won in the game – but there had been more than that in the pouch. I was so angry. How dare anyone rob a man who has stopped to help another? I concluded that I would be more careful from then onwards. Why bother helping others if I was going to lose out in the process? Perhaps I would have to learn to be a little more selfish.

That evening I made my excuses and slipped out of the inn. I didn't know but I suspected that the Boss would have disapproved of what I was about to do, and I had no wish to upset him or Han. Nor did I want a lecture about the dangers of gambling. I was sure that I knew what I was doing. Maybe I would be able to pack the job in. I was starting to get bored with the work anyway. Or, if things went well, perhaps I could buy him out?

The meeting place was a dingy room at the back of a scruffy little tavern in the roughest part of town. There were five of them in the room, plus Ben Obal. The others looked a fairly normal bunch –not the kind to start a fight if they lost. Anyway, I had only brought a small amount of money with me so if things turned nasty, I

The meeting place was a dingy room at the back of a scruffy little tavern in the roughest part of town

couldn't lose much. And even if it really did get rough, I was sure I could handle myself.

The game started. It was an old Hebrew game called "dreydl". I'd played it many times before in Carmel. A four-sided spinning top is used; each side has a letter from the Hebrew alphabet. When the dreydl is spun, if it lands on the right symbol, the person whose turn it is collects everything in the pot. Well, by the end of the evening I had made about half as much money as I'd earned in the previous few months working as a carpenter! I could hardly believe it. The other contestants cursed, swore, begged, borrowed, threw their hands into the air and called me the luckiest man in Israel. They seemed unable to believe what they had witnessed. Ben Obal stood at the back, a knowing smile on his face.

When the evening was over, he came forward,

"Same time next week, then?"

"Oh, I don't know", I said. "I mean, lightning doesn't strike in the same place twice, does it? It was my turn this evening; it might be someone else's next week."

"But, Hez, you're a natural." Again, that generous, encouraging smile. "I've never seen anyone as talented. Look, why not try one more week? The stakes will be higher. And it has to be said, it's poor form to win once and then walk away. Bad manners. Some haven't got the courage, but something tells me you're different from the rest."

The following week was a strange one. Work was busy, so I had little time to dwell on what had happened that evening. But somehow, I couldn't shake the feeling that I was on to something good. If I could win again – and if the stakes were higher – then maybe I could make my break sooner and move on. Looking back, I know my mind wasn't on my work. I realise that I made mistakes. It was hardly surprising when, on the Friday afternoon, the Boss called me over. He wanted to talk to me about my work. I'd made an error – used the wrong wood for a set of shelves – and he was going to be out of pocket. Unsurprisingly, he wasn't pleased.

"What's got into you this week, lad? Are you in love or something?"

"Give me a break, Boss" I pleaded, a smile on my face. "It's only one mistake. I mean it's not the end of the world, is it? Didn't you ever make mistakes when you were young?"

Straight away, I knew I'd gone too far. I will never forget that look on his face. He wasn't just angry; he was disappointed and hurt. He'd treated me so well since I'd arrived in the city. He'd shown me kindness and patience. All he wanted me to do was apologise, but I'd refused to do so, and he was backed into a corner. At first I wasn't sure what he would do. He seemed to be trying to compose himself. Suddenly I was aware that the rest of the workshop had become unnaturally quiet. It was then that he stood up.

"Just get out of my sight", he shouted. His voice rose to a high-pitched scream, and his face went a deep crimson colour. "I don't want to see you for the rest of the day. Do you hear me? Clear off, now! Go on, get out of here!" If I had spoken back to him, I think he would have knocked me out cold. I'd never seen him like this before.

I turned and walked away. As I did so, one of the other men stepped in front of me. He spoke quietly, but was clearly desperate for me to take on board what he was about to say.

"What's the matter with you? Just tell him you're sorry and it won't happen again. Come on Hez, grow up!"

"Get out of my way", I said, pushing past him. I left the workshop and raced back to the inn. I grabbed my tent – the one I had carried so proudly when I had left Carmel – and the various other items of value I had brought with me or bought since my arrival in the city, and went and sold them. I then went back to the inn, cleared out my last few remaining possessions, retrieved and counted all of my money from the place beneath the floorboards, and headed out.

Within three hours I was there again, round the table in the tavern with Ben Obal at my side and the other five men, clearly hoping to win back some of what they had lost the week before. This time we played a dice game called "goral". Again, I could do no wrong. And again, the others called me all the names under the sun. Two of them got up from the table in anger and stormed out, only to return a few minutes later.

Halfway through we took a break. Ben Obal had stayed out of the game. He came to me, speaking in a whisper,

"This is where it gets really interesting, my friend. You've got them in the palm of your hand. Now – don't give up – they're yours for the taking. They will bet all sorts of crazy sums, just hold your nerve and you're home and dry. And remember", he said, his face very close to mine, "don't let them bully you. They'll be bluffing. This is your night. One more win and you'll be set up for life."

We had been playing for about another half an hour when the tide began to turn. I suddenly started to lose. And the stakes were big – really big. Within about two hours I was down to my last few coins. I needed to roll two sixes. I agreed to be "bankrolled" – to take out a loan. I was sure I couldn't lose. And if I won just this one, I would be back where I had started from. I could walk away solvent. Then all I would have to do is build my bridges with the Boss, and I could pick up where I had started. I rolled the five dice. Two fives, a three and a one. And only one six. I had lost, big time. I had, very literally, nothing left to my name except the clothes I was wearing. More than that – I owed money to these men. When I did the sums, I realised that if I worked for a whole year and gave them everything, I would still only just be free.

For a few moments I sat there in silence, my heart racing. I wasn't quite sure what to do next. Ben Obal, who had been at my side throughout, sat with me. I wondered at first if he would agree to cover my debt. I even thought about making a dash for it. But I was the wrong side of the room. I'd never make it to the door. It was then that Ben stood up quickly and left the room. In less than two minutes he was back, and this time he wasn't alone. He had with him two of the biggest men I've ever seen. Both had shaved heads. They didn't look like Israelites

– Syrians, maybe, or Hittites? They certainly didn't look friendly.

"Now then, my friend", he fixed me with a cold stare, "what are we going to do about this little ... problem of yours?"

"Look, Ben, I've been set up. Those dice were loaded. I mean, how could I have done so well early on and then ...?"

Ben Obal cut in quickly:

"Now listen to me, you pathetic little country boy. We had a perfectly good game going here and you lost. You owe these gentlemen big time and, let me tell you this, you will pay up. They're not in the habit of making charitable donations."

I sat there, stunned. I was about to plead for time when suddenly Ben gave a signal and one of the hired musclemen grabbed me. Within seconds I was outside, being kicked and punched to within an inch of my life. I tried fighting back but got nowhere. One of them had a wooden club. The other had a leather whip. After what seemed to be about five minutes, they stopped hitting me, and I lay there in the filth, with blood streaming from my mouth, my hands, and a gash above my right eye. I was sure that one of my legs was broken. I couldn't feel my fingers. Ben Obal walked over to me. He crouched down beside me and pushed his face close to mine. He spoke very slowly, very menacingly,

"Forty-eight hours. That's how long you've got, Carmelite. We know where you live and work. And don't try heading back to Carmel. We'll be watching the road. Remember: forty eight hours. After that … well, I might have to stop being so friendly."

He gave me one last, massive kick in the stomach, and walked away. At that point I passed out. My final memory is of Ben Obal and the other men laughing, leaving me there, with more than just my clothes in tatters. I had lost everything.

Chapter 5

Redemption

I HAVE no idea how long I was out cold. Two hours? Three hours? Maybe more. When I did come round, my head felt as though it was exploding. My entire body screamed in agony. I was sure that every rib was broken. Slowly, painfully, I managed to stand up. The whole world seemed to be spinning. I had to hang on to the doorpost of the nearest house and wait for things to settle down. When they did, I decided to see if I could walk. After two steps I went straight over, and lay there, flat on my face, gasping for breath, racked with pain. I reached out, and found something, lying there at the side of the road. It felt like some sort of stick – possibly the club that had been used to beat me. With a great effort, I got up again and used the stick to support me. Very gingerly, I hobbled back towards the deserted marketplace. Nobody was about. Thankfully, Ben Obal and his gang had left. For the time being at least, I was safe.

At the side of the area where the market stalls had stood during the day there was a large water butt. It had rained steadily during the previous couple of days, so it was almost full. I managed to reach it and plunged my head right in. The pain was indescribable, but I had to try to clear my mind – and, at the very least, clean up some of these cuts. Once I had scraped off as much of the dirt as I could, and with most of the bleeding stopped, I started to think a little more clearly.

Obviously I had been set up. The more I thought about it, the more it made sense. Ben Obal (if that even was his name) had played me, right from the very start. Those three lads who couldn't work out which cup the coin was beneath – they were probably working for him. It was his way of snaring me – of reeling me in. I had taken the bait, and been caught, just like a fish in a Galilean's net.

The other men at the table in the filthy tavern? They were almost certainly in on it as well. They let me win until the stakes were high, and then took me for everything I had, and more. Had he stolen my money when he hugged me, the first day we met? No, I don't think so. But that incident when the old lady fell over and I helped her up – maybe that was also part of the act? Was that when my money was taken, perhaps by one of his lads? And what of his story of having been a tanner and caring for a sick uncle in Hebron? Almost certainly, complete and utter rubbish. Oh, what a fool I'd been! How could I possibly have been so gullible? I suppose I wasn't the first, and I certainly wouldn't be the last, but why couldn't I see what was happening? Nobody wins as many times as I had ... unless there's something going on. I looked up into the night sky and cursed myself.

"You idiot!" I said out loud. "You absolute, complete and utter idiot."

I had to decide what to do. I didn't feel I could go back to the inn. Not after what I had said to the Boss. They would know by now that I had cleared my room and might even have let it out to another man.

There was certainly no way I could raise the kind of money that Ben Obal was demanding. And even if I could, I would have been reluctant to pay him one more shekel. I don't mind losing, as long as it's fair. But he had to be the biggest con man in Israel's history. And, assuming that he meant what he'd said, I had forty-eight hours. After that, without my having any way to pay, he and his hired thugs would come after me, and that would be the end.

I concluded that there was only one option open to me. I would have to leave Hebron and get as far away from the city as possible. Head off into the hill country. Live off the land. I'd done it before, and I could do it again. There's no way Ben Obal would follow me there, surely? A man like that needs to be in the city streets, lining up his next victim to fleece.

With a struggle, I made my way to the city gates. They were closed, of course. The great wooden doors were barred at sunset, and weren't opened again until the cockerels started crowing. I gazed up at the sky and guessed that I had about two hours to wait. I lay down in the darkness, thankful that at least it was a dry night. I waited for the dawn to break.

When the doors of the city were opened by the watchman, I saw a look of complete astonishment in his eyes.

"What on earth has happened ...?"

By then I'd already hobbled through. I was in no mood to discuss what had gone on. For all I knew he was part of Ben Obal's gang as well. Nor did I want the Boss or Han to see me like this – I felt too ashamed. I just wanted to leave Hebron and never come back. I didn't know much of the surrounding area well, but knew that the road to the south led to Beersheba. It was about thirty miles away. I had no intention of reaching that city. Who knows how many men Ben Obal had in his employ? Maybe he worked the markets there as well? No, I wanted to get as far from Hebron as I could – to be away from civilisation – and perhaps, to lie down and rest. Just in case the watchman was in league with Ben Obal, I began on the road to Carmel. Then, when I was out of sight of the city, I cut across country and picked up the Beersheba road.

I had been travelling for about a mile when two men passed me, coming the other way. One was riding a donkey. I saw them look at me, and noted the astonishment in their eyes. I was a bit surprised when they turned round, then drew up alongside me. The one who had been riding the ass got off.

"Who did this to you?" he asked.

Initially, I refused to answer. He could have been one of Ben Obal's men, pretending to be concerned. I walked on. The man refused to give up:

"Let me help you, please."

I saw then that he was about sixty years old. His hair and beard were grey, but his skin was smooth and clear, making him look younger. I wasn't sure, but I thought he looked vaguely familiar. He wore a large, grey cloak with a blue border. It was bound in the centre by a broad leather belt. His accent wasn't local – northern, possibly. I paused to catch my breath. When I looked up I saw he was holding out a water skin to me.

"Here, have some of this. You look as though you need it."

I took the water bottle and drank. After a few seconds I gave him the skin back.

"Thank you, sir", I gasped. "Thank you. You're a good man."

"Here", he said, "hold your hands out." He poured some more of the water onto them.

"Rinse your face; you'll feel a bit better. And keep the bottle. I've got two more of these at home."

There was definitely something about him – something I was sure I had seen or heard before. I couldn't quite put my finger on it. Maybe he had been in the carpenter's shop?

"Look", he said, "we're heading up to Hebron, then to Ramah. You can ride the ass if you wish, and we'll take you with us."

"Oh no." I replied. "Anywhere in the world but Hebron. I'll just carry on towards Beersheba. I'll be all right."

"I understand." Although he didn't say, I suspected he knew exactly what had gone on. He had the air of a man of great perception.

He paused for a second, then reached out and, very gently, placed his hand on my shoulder:

"I'll pray for you, my son. Take care."

I was about to leave when the man reached into the bag hanging from the saddle of the ass. He handed me some figs and cheese, wrapped in a cloth. I was stunned. I had to bite back the tears. In the last twenty-four hours I had seen the very worst and very best of human nature. On the one hand, vile, deceitful, hate-filled depravity, and on the other, genuine, caring, self-sacrificing goodness. I thanked him once more and moved on. Chewing that food was painful – but the taste was fantastic.

I stumbled on. I passed a couple of men, who gazed at me with amazement. I thought one of them was from Hebron. Yes, I'm sure he worked in the potter's shop. I hoped that he wouldn't tell everyone there that he had seen me like this. It was about an hour afterwards that I came to a clearing and found some wild olive trees. The fruit wasn't particularly tasty, but at least it was fresh and there was plenty of it. I could hear the sound of running water and managed to locate a brook, hidden in the undergrowth. I drank what remained in the bottle, then refilled it. I then removed what was left of my tattered cloak and stood there in just my tunic. I washed my arms and legs. There was blood everywhere.

He handed me some figs and cheese, wrapped in a cloth

Thankfully – incredibly – I began to realise that my injuries were not as bad as I had first thought. Although I suspected that a few of my ribs were broken, that was probably it. Apart from that, just cuts and bruises – but lots and lots of them. The sun was up by now and, amazingly, it was a warm day – much better than the last couple of weeks. I wrapped my cloak around me and lay down. Within seconds was fast asleep.

I was awoken by the sound of men's voices. Immediately I knew I was in trouble. I recognised Ben Obal's 'dulcet tones'. He had clearly tracked me down, and was in no mood to let me off the debt. I lay still, but it didn't take long for his hired morons to find me. They were the same ones who had attacked me the night before. They picked me up and carried me down to where their leader was standing, together with another four men. I recognised at least two of them from the tavern. They dropped me on the ground, and I groaned in agony. For a few seconds, blows rained down on me from every side. Then they stopped, and Ben Obal, slowly, deliberately, placed his foot on my neck.

"Well, well, well. Trying to sneak off, are we? Trying to get away without paying your debts?" I could tell I was in big trouble. The hatred – the evil in his voice – there was no doubt about it; I'd come to the end.

"Do you think I don't know what's going on here?" he continued. "One of our friends saw you leave the city early on. Pathetic. Totally pathetic."

"Please", I gasped, "give me time. You'll get your money."

"Give him time, he says." I could hear the disbelief in his voice. The other men were laughing. "Time to get to Beersheba where you think you'll be safe? Time to recruit some of your stupid little friends from Carmel so you can fight back? Well, boy, this is the real world. And time is something that you have very little of."

It was then that I heard the sound of running feet. Ben Obal removed his foot from my neck, and I looked up. Into the clearing had come a group of three men. All of them young and athletic, and all with their cloaks tied up around the tops of their legs, to aid them in running. They didn't appear to be armed but it was hard to tell. I didn't know whether they were more friends of Ben, soldiers belonging to King Saul, guards from a nearby town or passing travellers. One of them spoke to Ben Obal,

"What's going on here then?"

"Nothing you need to concern yourself with, sir." It was Ben's 'friendly' voice, honed to perfection to assure everyone that nothing was amiss – that this was a perfectly normal, everyday occurrence.

"Just a bit of business with this gentleman here."

"A bit of business?" The man sounded surprised. "It looks as if you've already done your business and this one's been beaten senseless. I assume you are responsible for this?"

One of his men spoke up next. There was desperation in his voice,

"My lord, we must go. You know what the reports said. The king's men are nearby."

The first man turned to him. He spoke with great authority and, I suspected, a degree of frustration:

"Go? Go – and leave this man to the tender mercies of these animals? Never. You know my policy. If I can save one who is lost, I will do so." He turned to Ben Obal, "Now, let him go."

Ben gave a signal and one of his henchmen came at him, but despite the fact he must have been about a foot taller than the newcomer, the big man was down, screaming in agony before he knew what had hit him. I'd been involved in plenty of fights in my life and seen countless more, but this was something else. The man turned to Ben Obal again. This time his voice carried a hint of anger,

"Move away from him. Now. I won't ask you again."

After a few seconds, Ben and his team stepped aside and the man, with great tenderness, lifted me from the floor, and carried me away from them. He then turned back to my nemesis,

"If you dare to follow us, I will kill you. You have been warned. Now – get back to Hebron."

I was too tired – and too surprised to say anything. The three men walked back up the hill and then forked right into the heart of the woods. One was at the front; their leader was in the centre with me on his back. The other one brought up the rear. I was astounded by the pace they were able to maintain, especially as one was carrying another man. Yet they didn't slow down – not until we had been travelling for about half an hour. Then they stopped, and I was laid gently on the ground. My saviour removed his cloak and covered me up.

"Be back in a few minutes", he said, quietly. "Just stay here. Don't make a sound."

I had no idea what was happening. Much as I would have liked to join my rescuers, I was far too weak to have been of any use. About a quarter of an hour later, I heard the sound of footsteps. I looked up and saw the three travellers standing there again. I realised then that they had been checking to see if they had been followed. The leader bowed down upon his knees. I wasn't sure what he was doing, but it soon became clear that he was offering a silent prayer of thanks. We were safe. I was safe.

I didn't know it at the time, but that was the most important day of my entire life. Everything which had happened to me previously had been leading up to that incident. Everything afterwards would be influenced by it.

One moment my life was as good as over. Then these complete strangers had appeared out of nowhere and rescued me. I had been snatched away from almost certain death and carried to a place of security and love. It would, in fact, be the pattern for many, many more men and women in Israel in the following days. Indeed I would, on occasions, do for others what this man had done for me. It would take me a while to see it, but Israel's God – the Mighty One of Abraham, Isaac and Jacob – had reached out to me and pulled me back from the abyss through this one, amazing, courageous, faithful man. My life in his service was about to begin.

Chapter 6

My Lord David

THE THREE men hugged and then spoke very quietly for just a few seconds. I was able to make out only a small amount of what was said. I recall the name of Saul being mentioned, and one of them said they needed to move on. Their leader came over and kneeled down beside me. He placed his hand on my shoulder.

"How are you feeling, then?"

I smiled. "A lot better than I was before you turned up. Look, there's so much I need to say ..."

I didn't get the chance to go any further. The man cut in,

"Not just now, my friend. There'll be plenty of time for questions later. We've got a few miles to travel and need to reach somewhere safe before the sun sets, if we can. You are welcome to come with us – but the choice is yours."

There really was no choice to make. I had to remain with these men.

"I would be honoured to come with you", I said, and the other man smiled.

"I hoped you'd say that. Do you feel able to walk?"

"Yes, I think so."

I stood up and he supported me. I took some deep breaths, waiting for the muddled feeling in my head to pass. Looking back, I remember that at the time it seemed like some crazy dream. But there was no doubt about it, this was really happening.

We walked, slowly at first, through the forest. The men obviously knew the area well. Just when I thought we were coming to a dead end, they would head off to the right or left and find a new path. When it became clear that I could walk faster, they upped the pace, and we continued our journey. I remember thinking that we were probably heading south, but I really wasn't sure. We paused after about an hour, and I was asked if I felt able to go on. I ached like mad. My ribs were killing me, and my right leg was throbbing, but I didn't want to let on. I had no wish to appear weak in front of these men, and I knew that they had to avoid being captured – and that meant staying together and moving on.

Shortly afterwards the man in front held up his hand and we all froze. I suspected that there were others in the forest – soldiers from Saul's army perhaps, or even Ben Obal's men. I was wrong. A magnificent deer walked calmly through a clearing, only a few feet in front of us. Silently, the man reached for his bow and arrows and, within seconds, the deer was down. For those who have

A magnificent deer walked calmly through a clearing, only a few feet in front of us

no experience of this kind of lifestyle I imagine this may sound gory – cruel even. But, living in the wild, it was just a way of life. We had to eat, and that meant tracking down wild animals like that deer. The man lifted it quickly on to his shoulders and we continued our journey.

The sun was about to set when we crossed a small brook. One of the men hooted like an owl, and we waited in silence. A few seconds later we heard another 'hoot' and continued walking. We had reached a large hedge, and the man in front moved some branches aside. As far as anyone would have known, this was just part of a deep, impenetrable forest – only wild animals about, and not many of those. And yet, when we walked through that gap in the undergrowth, I was totally amazed by the sight that greeted me.

There were tents. Fifty or more, all laid out in what was clearly a very precise order. People were milling about – men and women, young and old, and a few children. There were animals as well: about ten asses and a few sheep, goats and hens. At the far end of the enclosure a fire was burning, and the aroma of cooking wafted through the air. A number of large water pots stood nearby. A basic washing line was strung between two trees, with clothes of all shapes and sizes hanging on it. As I took in the sight, I was stunned by the level of organisation. This was no random collection of fugitives. This was like a mini city, and it was clear that every man and woman was playing a role, ensuring that things followed a defined pattern.

"Well, what do you think of the Kahal?" asked one of the men.

"The Kahal?" I asked.

"Yes, that's what we call this place. It means an assembly. We all came here for different reasons – but mostly because we needed somewhere safe, and we wanted to serve our Lord – and Almighty God."

Their "Lord", I assumed, was the man who had saved me. All around, people were greeting the members of our party. It was like a family gathering, and suddenly I felt a bit out of place. Well, that didn't last long. My saviour came up to me and asked me to join him for something to eat. I was aware that this was a great honour and was delighted to accept his invitation. One of the other men offered a prayer of thanks before the meal, and everyone concluded with a resounding "Amen". The food was simple but tasty, and there was enough for everyone. There were clearly some very capable cooks amongst the men and women in the group.

As the night wore on, I started to feel more and more at home amongst these people. One of the men produced a basic harp and they started singing. The songs were all psalms. A few of the phrases sounded vaguely familiar to me. As I didn't know many of the words or any of the tunes, I was unable to join in, but I do recall being stunned by the beauty of that music. The male and female voices harmonised so wonderfully. No choir in any of the courts of King Saul could have sounded better. Maybe it was because I was so tired, but I found myself wiping away a tear on more than one occasion.

As the singing concluded, a final prayer was offered. I hadn't finished a day with a prayer in a long, long time – not since Mum had died – but I bowed my head and listened to the words of one of the older men. He glorified God, thanking Him for keeping us safe during the day, for the love of the Kahal, for food and clothing, and for what he called "the Hope of Israel". He praised the Almighty for "new arrivals", and asked that more might come to join us. I knew immediately what he meant. He was talking about me. At this point I was totally overcome by the emotion of it all. The man closest to me reached out a comforting arm and placed it round my shoulders. Finally, the elder prayed for safety through the night, and for the Messiah to come.

My saviour, who was very clearly the leader of the group, came over to me.

"Time for bed, my friend", he said, leading me to one of the tents. "I'm normally up early, so please come and find me tomorrow and I will be happy to answer all of your questions. My tent is the one nearest to the entrance there."

He pointed to a tent which looked exactly like the others, but stood immediately in front of the 'gap' in the hedge through which we had entered earlier in the evening. I knew straight away why it was there. If there were any unwanted 'visitors', he would be the first line of defence. He was like a shepherd, and these people were his flock. He turned to me again:

"Normally around four or five men share a tent, but you'll be by yourself this evening, until you've settled in – and till you've decided if you want to remain with us."

This last comment left me a bit taken aback. Why would anyone ***not*** want to stay here? Why would I want to live anywhere else, especially after what had been done for me? I think my saviour read my thoughts,

"Don't worry about that now. Just get a good night's sleep and we'll chat in the morning, God willing."

Again, I was amazed by his care – his perceptiveness. I guessed he was only a few years older than me, but he was so mature, so knowledgeable, so kind and brave. What a man. What an amazing man!

By now I was totally exhausted. Fleeing from Hebron, the second beating at the hand of Ben Obal's men, the long journey, the emotion of the evening with the words of the psalms and prayers – finally it had all caught up with me. My bed was basic but comfortable: animal skins covering soft leaves. Within seconds I was asleep.

When I woke the following day, I realised that I must have slept for well over twelve hours. I looked out of the tent door and saw that the Kahal was well and truly 'awake'. Everywhere I looked, people were at work. Some had clothes in baskets or barrels. Others were preparing food or tending to the animals. Two men at the end of the encampment were chopping wood. The sun was high in the sky; I guessed it was about noon.

By the side of my 'bed' someone had placed clean clothes: a tunic, a robe, a leather belt and sandals. There was also a bowl of water and towel. These people were fantastic! I washed and dressed, and stepped out into the bright sunshine. Those nearest to me all turned and smiled, welcoming me. One of the older men came up and hugged me.

"Welcome, my son, welcome!" He had a friendly, genuine voice and a lovely, rounded southern accent. "I thank God in heaven for bringing you to us."

I realised then that this was the same man who had given the concluding prayer the previous evening. Again, I felt myself welling up.

"Thank you", I said. "Thank you for everything."

It was then that I saw my saviour coming towards me. He had clearly been out of the camp early in the morning. Maybe hunting. Possibly checking that there were no enemies around. The people all welcomed him with great respect and love.

"Good morning, my lord. May God bless you today and always."

He smiled when he saw me.

"Now then", he said, "how about that chat?"

We sat down outside his tent and one of the women brought us food and drink. He thanked her, and I began to eat. Then suddenly I looked up and saw that he hadn't started. I felt a sudden pang of conscience. He hadn't offered a prayer. I had been so accustomed to eating without giving thanks that I had forgotten that this was the way of things for so many in Israel. I waited for him to thank God for the food. After he had concluded, I apologised, and he smiled. When "breakfast" was over, he turned to me.

"So, tell me all about yourself. What's your name, first of all?"

"Hezrai. But people normally call me Hez." I felt I could go no further without talking about the events of the previous day.

"Look", I said, "I have to thank you for everything you did yesterday. I don't know what would have happened if you hadn't turned up and saved me." (Actually I knew exactly what would have happened – Ben Obal's men would almost certainly have beaten me to a pulp and thrown my battered body into some ditch.)

He laughed. "That's all right. I'm just pleased we came along when we did. I've met others in similar circumstances. I genuinely believe that it was meant to be; I was guided there by God. So, Hez, what do you think of this place?"

I gasped. "Absolutely amazing. It's unlike anything I've ever seen before."

"That's good to hear. This is a pattern, you know, for the whole of the country. But more about that later. Tell me about yourself."

I told him about my childhood and growing up in Carmel. I explained how my Dad had been killed at Gaza, fighting for King Saul. I said that my Mum and sisters had died when I was young, and I had lived with my uncle and aunty. We spoke about family life, and I mentioned Uncle Jed's drinking and how I had to get away. We chatted about Hebron and my work as a carpenter.

"So who were those men who had attacked you yesterday?"

I was almost too ashamed to admit how I knew Ben Obal, but I knew that, if I was going to stay here, I would have to be totally honest with this man.

"I ... I got into debt, gambling." I shook my head and sighed. "Such an idiot. I thought I was so clever, and then..."

"Let me guess: you had a few good wins, and then everything turned sour? You ended up with nothing and they got nasty?"

I was astonished. "How did you know?"

"Well, let's say you're not the first man to come to us having been through exactly the same experience. I can understand it entirely. Easily done."

Once more, his kindness and love shone through. Others would have condemned me for being stupid and greedy, but not my saviour. I had to know more about this group – and, most especially, about him.

"Who are you? The others call you their Lord. What is your name?"

"My name is David. I'm originally from Bethlehem."

David ... David. Where had I heard that name before? Then suddenly it hit me. I remembered what the Boss had said, that evening in the carpenter's shop. David was the name of the next king. Could this be the same man? I had to know.

"A wise man – one whom I loved and trusted – once told me that the next king of this land will be called by that name. I have to know – is this you?"

David paused for a few seconds and looked away. Then he turned back to me and fixed me with a stare which told me that this was a matter of real importance.

"Hez, before I tell you any more, I need to know that I can trust you. What we have here is very special. But I can't do anything which might jeopardize the safety of any man, woman or child in my care. So, do you give me your solemn word that what I tell you will remain in the confines of the Kahal until I tell you otherwise?"

Again, I felt myself welling up although I didn't really know why. Maybe it was because this great man was about to trust me with some vital information which could have a bearing on many others. He appeared to be willing to give me the opportunity to be united with him and those closest to him. I dropped to my knees before him.

"My lord", I said, wiping my eyes, "I vow before you here and now that I will never reveal anything confidential to those outside the Kahal. I give you my word as an Israelite."

He was clearly pleased with my decision. When I stood up he hugged me. I was amazed to see that there were tears in his eyes as well.

For the next few hours we sat and talked. He told me about his early life in Bethlehem in Judah. He was the youngest of a large family. His older brothers looked down on him and he was left to care for the sheep, taking them anywhere he could find pasture. He had occasionally killed mountain lions and bears as he protected the flock.

One day, he was called back to the family home and the prophet Samuel was there. In the presence of his father and brothers, the great seer anointed him with oil and declared that he would be the next king of Israel. Shortly afterwards he was summoned to stand before King Saul and played the harp in his presence. Then came the duel with Goliath.

"Goliath?" I asked. "Wasn't he the Philistine champion who was defeated by a ...?" My words trailed off. David smiled,

"By a young shepherd with a sling and stones?"

"That was you?"

"Yes. But before we go any further I have to mention something that you have probably already worked out for yourself. I worship Yahweh, the mighty God of Abraham, Isaac and Jacob. Serving Him is, without question, the most important thing in my life – as it is for most of those here. We seek to keep His laws and glorify Him in all that we do. This is why I defeated that Philistine. Not simply because I'm a decent shot with a sling – but because I went to meet the enemy in the name of Israel's God, and He was with me. He has blessed and kept me since my youth, and I believe He will continue to do so. And yes, one day He will make me ruler of this land, as foretold by Samuel."

"What about Saul?" I asked.

"King Saul is becoming more and more rebellious – and erratic. He is forever sending bands of soldiers to try to capture or kill me. But he is the Lord's anointed, and I have vowed that I will never kill him, so that I can seize the throne. He will fall in battle one day, I imagine. Only then can the kingdom be mine, by the grace of God."

"So what of Jonathan?" I asked. "Has he turned out like his father? Is that why the royal house has been rejected by God?"

I looked up and saw genuine sorrow in the eyes of David. He remained silent, looking down to the ground.

"Jonathan is nothing like his father whatsoever, Hez", he said very slowly, and with great feeling. "He is the finest man I've ever known. He is the greatest friend any man could ever ask for. Saul's royal house has been rejected because it is the will of the Almighty that another should reign – but, no, it is most certainly not because of any sin committed by Jonathan."

Suddenly I was full of remorse.

"I'm so sorry, my lord, I had no wish to ..."

"Don't worry, Hez. There are some in this nation who dare to mock or criticise Jonathan. They suggest that he is weak for not turning on me. But I know the truth, and I will never allow anyone to speak a word against him. I made a covenant with him and will do anything I can to care for him or his family. Like the people here – I will do all I can to protect them, no matter what."

I was stunned by these words. What an honour it must be to be part of this group! To have someone like this man looking out for you – caring for you – protecting you – sacrificing for you. It was almost too wonderful to take in.

For the rest of the day I helped out in the camp in any way I could. I chopped wood and fetched water from the brook. I helped in preparing the food and sharpened knives and tools.

As the sun began to set, David sought me out once again. He explained that it was time for me to decide what I wanted to do with my life.

"Do you want to be part of this group, Hez? The choice is yours. You don't have to stay. But if you choose to do so, you have to agree to abide by the rules of the camp. You must live in accordance with the laws of Israel's God."

I paused. I suddenly felt uncomfortable. I wanted more than anything to stay with David. But I didn't believe what he believed – or, perhaps, not yet.

"Oh my lord, I really want to be part of this ... it's just that ... well, I don't have your faith. I wish I could believe in a God as you do ... but I've experienced so much sadness. I don't know ... I find it hard to accept that a God who is the source of all good could also allow my parents to die when I was so young."

David, predictably, didn't condemn me or criticize. In a way, he appeared to appreciate my honesty. He placed a hand on my shoulder.

"Hez, I'm not asking you to pretend to be something you're not. You are welcome to stay here, but you must agree to abide by our laws – God's laws. Others have come to us just like you – uncertain, disillusioned, hurt, grief-stricken. They have also lost loved ones and have experienced all sorts of hardship. In time they have come to believe in our God and now they serve Him with all their hearts. Faith will come. I genuinely believe that. But it has to be your choice. So, would you like to stay with us?"

I knew the time had come to make a decision. In truth, there was really only one choice.

"My Lord David", I said. "I would be honoured if you would allow me to join you here at the Kahal."

Chapter 7

Fighting the good fight

OVER THE coming months I settled down to life in the Kahal and, despite the hardness of our existence, I came to feel very much at home. Living in a tent isn't always easy. I shared with four other men and, unsurprisingly, some of their habits got to me. I'm sure that some of the things I did and said caused just as much annoyance – but, working together for the same cause, we rarely fell out.

The group numbered around three hundred altogether, but others arrived all the time. Some, like me, had been in debt. Others were downcast, or distressed by the circumstances of life. I watched as David greeted them, caring for them as he had cared for me. He showed them how the Kahal worked, and allowed them time to settle in. He always ensured that they knew what we stood for, and how the laws and ways of Almighty God came first. Even though he was so busy, he made a point of speaking to each of us as regularly as possible. My respect and love for him grew day by day.

Work in the group was organised by three of the elders, under the ultimate guidance of David. Those in the first group were tasked with making or repairing tools, tents and other necessary items. Many were involved in preparing and cooking food, and in washing, mending or making clothes. Members of the second group made checks on the camp itself and the area nearby, ensuring that the borders were secure. Those appointed to serve in group three made up the "working parties" which were sent out, looking for supplies and checking for spies from Saul's army.

One afternoon some of the men had been practising their swordsmanship. We had hardly any genuine weapons. There had been very few 'real' swords in Israel for many years while the Philistines held the upper hand. We fashioned swords out of anything we could find. As a carpenter, I quickly found that my skills in shaping, refining and repairing these items were in great demand. That afternoon I was handed a weapon and challenged to defend myself against three other men. When, after around five minutes, my 'opposition' finally got the better of me, I looked up and noticed that David had been watching.

"Well done, Hez", he said, and hugged me. "I think you're ready to join us."

I was immediately conscious of the honour of this position. This was not a job for the young, weak or elderly. Those in a group had to be willing to travel great distances and fight, if necessary, even to the death.

And so, the following day, with David taking the lead, we left the Kahal and headed off into the forest.

It was the first time I'd been far from the safety of the camp for more than a few hours since I'd arrived. The other members of the party were Joab and Asahel – two of David's relations – and a man called Uriah. I later learned that he was a Hittite who had converted to the Hebrew faith. They were all of a similar age to me – maybe a couple of years older – but they seemed far more experienced in the ways of the world. Joab was the oldest; he was around David's age. He was one of the men who had been there when I had been rescued. I think he was the one who wanted to move on and was rebuked by David.

Initially, I wasn't sure where we were heading. I wondered if we would travel back towards Hebron, or to one of the other built-up areas. After a while it became clear we were heading north. We avoided the larger cities and towns altogether, travelling mostly during the evenings or very early in the morning, when there were fewer people around. When we needed to sleep we would find a cave or deserted sheepfold. One would be on watch, normally for around three or four hours. There were three watches per night. We had brought some food with us but would pick, and cook, anything we could find.

One morning I was alone with David. The others had remained back in the cave in which we had slept the previous night. We had heard reports of a large number of Saul's men being stationed in the area, and so had decided to avoid travelling as a group as much as possible, heading out only in pairs.

"I imagine this must be very different from anything you've experienced before", said David.

"I've done my share of camping out, my lord. I used to sleep in caves and home-made dens when I was younger. I wasn't always the most popular lad around, but I've never had people trying to capture or kill me. I suppose the others have been with you for many years; they seem so capable."

"Yes, they are", he replied. "All of them, great and mighty warriors. But, Hez, I need to warn you about getting too close to the wrong kind of people. Strictly between us, Joab is a lion in battle – one of the bravest men I've ever met and totally loyal to me, but he doesn't appear to have any interest in the really important things – those to do with the service of our God."

I was amazed. Joab was the first person to be chosen for scouting missions. In the short time I'd been in the group, I'd never seen anyone beat him in any sort of 'fight'. He seemed so confident. So capable. But it never crossed my mind to question his attitude in other areas.

David checked that we were not being followed.

"Joab is a man with his own agenda – his own rule book. He wants to be in control all the time. And, although I haven't seen him openly break any of the laws of God, he's never shown even the slightest indication that he loves such things. He doesn't join us in the singing, and he never listens to the reading of the law or asks questions of the elders. Maybe he'll change. I've known him since we were children. His mother is one of my sisters. I really hope that he will mature in time."

I had imagined that everyone within the Kahal would be mentally "as one", but this clearly wasn't the case. I thanked David for trusting me enough to share this information with me and determined to be wary of anything that Joab might ask me to do.

When it became clear that the guards from Saul's army had moved on, we continued north, finally arriving at a city called Nob. This was north-east of Jebus and was a priestly city. By this time all the food we had brought with us had gone. Had it been harvest time, we could have gleaned or picked fruit from the trees, but there was nothing about. I saw David speaking to one of the priests and, within a few minutes, he returned with bread for us. Joab ate his without a word of gratitude to David or a prayer to God. I knew better, and waited while Uriah offered a heartfelt, moving expression of thanks and praise, asking for continued guidance and that we might return home safely. This was the first time I had witnessed Joab's character up close. I saw the disappointment in David's eyes – and noted, with sadness, Joab's look of complete arrogance. Uriah must have seen my astonishment and a few minutes later he drew me to one side.

"In one of our sacred writings, we read that great men are not always wise", he said. "Joab is one of the greatest men I've ever known when it comes to wielding a sword in battle ... but he's no spiritual giant. He's nothing compared with our lord."

Before we left I heard David ask the chief priest for a sword. The few we had back at base were basic in the extreme – little more than wooden shafts sharpened to a point. The priest, whose name was Ahimelech, seemed unsure.

"We've only got one sword here. It's the one you took from the Philistine giant when you beheaded him."

"There's no other weapon like that one", said David. "Please, let me take it."

When it was handed over, I was amazed by what I saw. It wasn't just the size; it was the way it was made. Whoever had forged that weapon was a gifted man indeed. We were all allowed to hold it. I must admit, it was only then that I realized the magnitude of the victory that David had achieved over that Gentile. To kill a man who had carried this weapon was an awesome feat. We'd all heard about the giant from Gath – a man over nine feet tall – but, as I held that sword for myself, I finally appreciated what David had done when he did battle with him.

"My lord", said Joab, "you see that man lurking over there? He's an Edomite called Doeg. A vile, pathetic coward of a man. I've heard he works for Saul. He looks after his herds of cattle. What if he reports back, telling others that we were here? Surely we can't take the chance?"

"I won't kill a man unless he has broken one of the key laws of our God ... or unless he is a definite threat to us", replied David.

"Well, let me do it for you, my lord", said Joab. I could sense the frustration – the impatience in his voice. "After

... as I held that sword for myself,
I finally appreciated what David
had done ...

a few seconds alone with him, I'd soon have him begging for mercy."

"I've made my decision, Joab", replied David. "Don't speak to me about this again."

Once more, I saw the look of disdain in Joab's eyes. I knew he disagreed with David, but he had clearly decided against bringing the matter up again.

Once David had said his farewells to the priests in Nob, we began our journey back towards the south. We avoided Bethlehem altogether. Uriah had told me that there were a number of Saul's men stationed there permanently in case David tried to see his family.

On the way, we stopped at a brook outside the city of Tekoah. And almost immediately, I knew we were in trouble. David had sent Asahel ahead, and he returned almost immediately in a state of panic.

"Soldiers, my lord. About twelve of them. They're blocking the road out of the city and questioning the locals."

"Did they know you?" asked David.

"I can't be sure, but I think so."

We retreated a short distance until we found ourselves in a gap between two large, tall rocks. Smaller boulders lay on the ground and there were a few old bushes, providing more protection. Behind us was a valley, with no easy way down. Climbing the rock face without any ropes would have been just about impossible.

"Now we sit and wait", said David.

For a few minutes nothing happened. The silence was punctuated only by the sounds of nature: the call of birds and, way down below us, a river. Then, without warning, the attack commenced. Arrows flew from all directions and we took cover, thankful for those smaller rocks which lay at the foot of the cliffs.

For the first time in many years – certainly since my Mum had died – I decided to pray. I looked round at the others and it was clear that David and Uriah were already doing this. I gazed down, feeling shame that I had never thought to pray before and closed my eyes for a few seconds.

"Almighty Father of Abraham, Isaac and Jacob ... please be with us now. Please keep my lord David in safety, I pray."

After a few seconds of silence, I heard David's voice ringing out, loud and clear, with great authority,

"Servants of King Saul and Abner – this is David of Bethlehem. I know you have been sent to take me and that you wish to obey your master. But I have done nothing wrong, and I will not let you capture me or any of my men. We will fight – even to the death if necessary. You have been warned. Leave now or face the consequences."

Shortly afterwards, the soldiers came at us. They were quick, far better equipped than we were and with fine, sturdy armour. But we were organised and had David as our guide and leader – a man bearing the sword of the enemy giant.

In that enclosed space they could only come at us one or two at a time. As they did, we were able to fend off their advances. The first man was taken down by David with a single blow, and his sword seized. In a matter of minutes, another three lay on the ground. One man, I suspected, was dead. The others were injured. We gagged them and tied their hands behind their backs. By now we all had swords, and readied ourselves for the next assault.

One man leapt at me and, for a couple of seconds, I was on my back. I managed to avoid the spear as he attempted to impale me to the ground, and scrambled back to my feet. He came at me again, but this time I was able to wrench the spear from his grasp and cast it aside. He reached for his dagger, but I took him down with a stroke of the sword and he lay very still on the ground.

I looked up and saw two men wrestling with Uriah. One was about to strike. Without a second thought I leapt on the first man, hauling him off. We fell to the ground and rolled together. As he reached for his weapon, I was able to grab a large stone which lay nearby and with just one blow he was out cold. The second man was still wrestling with Uriah when Joab hurled a spear with great power and accuracy, and the man fell.

A few feet away, David and Asahel were engaged in a fight with four of Saul's men. I was amazed by their speed and courage. They fought back-to-back, so the enemy could only come from one direction. In no time at all, they were victorious. After a few seconds, David spoke up,

"I think that's it, my brothers."

He hugged us all.

"Well done today – Joab, Asahel, Uriah, Hez – all of you, brave and noble warriors in the service of Almighty God."

"My lord", asked Asahel, "what about the prisoners?"

"We leave them here", replied David. "We never take a life unless there is no other option. These men are Israelites. I hate having to kill any man – especially one of God's people. But it was them or us, and we did all we could to avoid this conflict. Now, my brothers, let us pray."

We knelt on the ground and David offered a few words of praise, thanks and love. He prayed for peace in God's land and for our safe passage back to the Kahal. He made mention of the coming of the Messiah and what he called "the true promised seed of Abraham". He thanked God for the Hope of Israel.

As we got up to go, that last phrase stuck in my mind. I had heard the same expression a number of times during my time with David. "The Hope of Israel" – what did it mean? What was this great hope which seemed so very important to so many in the camp? One thing was certain – I had to know more. David's supreme self-confidence came not from the fact he was a great, mighty, capable warrior, but from his faith in God – his belief that, come what may, the Almighty One of Israel was his guide and He had promised great things in His word. This was David's hope. And the more I thought about it, the more I realised that I wanted to share this same hope as well.

Chapter 8

The Hope of Israel

AFTER WE had taken the weapons and food from Saul's men we began our journey home. As we passed nearby the city of Tekoah, we spotted a young lad, and David called for him to be taken. When Joab brought him before us the youngster was, understandably, terrified.

"Don't worry my son", said David, crouching down beside him. "We're not going to hurt you; I give you my word. My name is David of Bethlehem. Although I have done nothing wrong, some soldiers were sent by King Saul to capture me, and there was a skirmish over by the two great rocks. There are a number of men lying injured, and they need help. I don't want any of them to die. Most of them will be fine, but they will need care for a few days. Now – can I trust you to go back to the city and tell the elders about this?"

"Yes, sir." The boy was still in a state of shock.

"Good man", replied David, and hugged him. "Have some of this." He handed over some of the food we had taken from the soldiers and a couple of coins.

The lad scampered off towards the city and we quickly picked up the road heading south towards Hebron. Uriah and I were at the back of the group. He was clearly used to this kind of thing and checked that we weren't being followed regularly. Asahel – who was the quickest runner I had ever seen in my entire life – went on ahead, reporting back that the coast was clear.

As we rounded a corner, we came to a grove where around a dozen trees grew by a river. David raised his hand and we all stopped. There were a few men ahead, and a number of asses tied up. One of the men was standing; he had the appearance of a teacher. The others sat before him, obviously hanging on his every word. I wasn't sure whether we would avoid them altogether or go over and speak with them. What happened next took me completely by surprise. David fell to his knees and gave an audible prayer of thanks to God for allowing him, as he put it, "to meet my lord once again."

The 'teacher' then looked up and gave a cry of joy. The other men looked round with a degree of surprise.

"Just give me ten minutes, my son David, and then we can speak, God willing."

"Thank you, my lord. Thank you."

The teacher then concluded his 'lesson'. I was still astonished by this. Who was this man, and why did David regard him so highly? I turned to Asahel,

"Who is this?"

"Don't you know? Oh, Hez, you must be one of the few men in Israel who doesn't know Samuel."

There were a few men ahead, and a number of asses tied up

"Samuel? Well, I know who he is. He's the great seer who teaches in different cities. People flock to hear him. I was taken as a young lad to one of his talks, though I can't really remember anything he said."

"Our lord has spent many hours with him, being instructed in the law", explained Asahel. "They've made all sorts of plans for the organisation of the kingdom."

By now, Samuel had concluded his teaching session and had called us over to him. As soon as I saw him, I also dropped to my knees. This was the very man I had met on the road to Beersheba when I had fled from Hebron – the man who had given me the water bottle and food!

We listened as David relayed the account of the previous few hours to Samuel. The seer appeared saddened, but not shocked. He agreed that David needed to move on and get back to the safety of the Kahal as soon as possible. Before we departed, David introduced us all to the seer. One by one we bowed before him. When my turn came, I heard David's voice,

"This is Hezrai, or Hez, a Carmelite. A new recruit. A great warrior, and a faithful and loving companion."

Samuel placed his hand on my shoulder.

"My son, I feel we've met before."

"Yes, my lord", I replied, struggling to hold back the tears. "A few months ago I was on the road from Hebron to Beersheba and you kindly helped me."

Samuel seemed unable to recall the incident. I went on,

"You gave me a water skin and some food. You said you would pray for me."

“Ah, yes. You had been involved in some sort of fight, I think? I prayed to the Almighty, my child, that you would find sanctuary and love ... that someone would care for you and teach you about our God and His ways. You met one of the few men in Israel able to provide these things for you. Truly the angels of our Lord are always at work, caring for His children. Stay with David, Hez. Trust him – and you will enjoy greatness at his side, one day.”

After David had said his final farewells to the seer, we moved on. We had travelled for about a mile when Uriah turned to me,

“Hez, you saved my life today. I thank you my brother, and I thank Almighty God for bringing you to us.”

“I’m sure you would have done the same for me”, I said. “But, Uriah, I have to ask, what brought you to Israel? You have such belief – such certainty that Israel’s God is holy and true. I wish I could share your faith.”

For the rest of the journey we spoke about Uriah’s life, his relationship with David, and his faith. He told me how he had first met our lord. Mostly we spoke about Israel’s God and the way Uriah believed He had worked in his life.

When he told me the story of his childhood I was dumbstruck. He had experienced far more hardship than me in his early years. His family had been brutally murdered in front of his eyes by Syrian warriors, and he had been made to work as a slave. In time, he had been sold to a family of Israelites. Although they had treated him better, he was still only a bond-servant. Then he was bought by another man from Israel and granted his freedom. That man was one of the elders at the camp, Ahithophel. He was the one who taught him about the mighty God of Israel and gave him his new name: Uriah, or "flame of Yah".

"I keep hearing the phrase "hope of Israel", I said. "And people talking about Abraham's seed. What's this all about?"

"The hope of Israel is the hope we all share", said Uriah. "A hope that will be realised at some time in the future. The land of Israel – and in time the whole world – will be transformed. Although I was born a Hittite, I have been adopted into the nation of Israel and allowed to become part of these immense things. God's promises to the fathers of the nation even speak of this. Abraham was told that, through one who would come, even Gentiles can be saved."

I turned to Uriah, "So when will this time of transformation come?"

"Hez, we don't know when it will happen but ultimately even sin and death will be no more. The Lord God, the mighty one of Israel, has promised that His faithful servants will be granted immortality one day – made like His angels. A race of immortal beings will serve and glorify Him on earth forever. This is the hope of Israel. This is the hope which I embraced."

"What about the seed?" I asked. "If the seed is the one who will come, why not say "son" or "child"?

"A seed is all about potential. I'm sure you have sowed seeds in the ground in the past, Hez?"

I laughed. "Of course. Different kinds of herbs – or wheat or barley."

"Right. You sow a seed which appears to be dead. Then it comes to life, and lots more grows. One small seed – but a plant or a tree springs up, from which many more seeds are produced. The anointed one, or Messiah, will be just one man. He will die – but he will be restored to life again. Others will serve and follow him. They will all be members of that one great seed. Many and yet one."

My mind went back to Carmel and the lessons my Mum used to teach me. I was sure she had said something about this.

"I seem to recall the seed being compared with different things", I said.

"You're right", replied Uriah. "The seed is like the stars in the sky – the sand on the seashore – or the dust of the earth. Think about the stars. They are glorious to behold. And beyond number – lots of stars in one sky. That's what the seed is like. Wonderful – and so many that no man can count them."

I thought about that first night, when I had left Carmel. I remembered those beautiful, twinkling fires which filled the night sky. I knew that the sacred writings of the nation mentioned the stars and how they represented something else but, at the time, I wasn't sure what that was. Now it was starting to make sense.

Uriah went on,

"The individual grains of sand are far too many to number, at least by any mortal man or woman. But

Almighty God knows the exact number of grains on any beach, and He knows who are His. He has called you, Hez – just as He called me. I'm certain of it. He has brought you to us. Now, you have a choice. You can be like Joab, a fearsome warrior, or like our lord, David – a fearsome warrior and a mighty man. Mighty because of his faith."

For the rest of the journey we travelled in silence. Those last words – together with the events of the day – had left me stunned. If a man like Uriah could see it, then why couldn't I? He was a Gentile by birth and had experienced far more sadness than I had, yet he had embraced the things of Israel and was a man of awesome faith. And he demonstrated this by the way he acted and spoke. He was just like his lord.

I remembered Samuel's words – how he had prayed for me, and I thought of how I had been rescued by David a short while afterwards. I recalled that simple prayer that I had uttered back there outside Tekoah, and how it had been answered. We had survived, against all the odds. The more I thought about it, the more I realised that the God whose existence I had denied for so long had, without question, been at work in my life. He had brought me to David. He had cared for me, protected me and loved me. And He was challenging me to serve and glorify Him.

Chapter 9

Fugitives, part one

OVER THE coming days my love for David and those in the Kahal grew stronger all the time. Uriah was like an older brother to me – kind, brave, funny – but never afraid to tell me if I stepped out of line. Each day there were 'classes' where members of the group could sit and learn from others – specifically the elders. These groups were entirely optional. Men like Joab and his brother Abishai never attended. At first this surprised me but, after a while, I came to accept it. Others were there only occasionally. Some would come every day for a couple of weeks, and then their initial interest faded. I did my best to attend as often as possible and found that my love for God's law and His ways, and my appreciation of His greatness increased every day.

As soon as we had arrived back in the camp, I had asked Uriah about Ahithophel – the man who had freed him from bondage and taught him about the hope of Israel. He introduced him to me as soon as we were both free. Initially, I have to admit, I was a bit disappointed!

Physically, he looked just like any other man. Grey hair and beard. Not particularly tall or strong. But ... what a mind! I was stunned by his knowledge – but also by his humility. He never made anyone feel stupid, even though he was so very wise.

On one occasion I confused Cain and Abel; I had convinced myself that it was Cain who was faithful, and that Abel had killed him. Ahithophel corrected me – but with great kindness and patience. And in doing so he also explained the account of Adam and Eve's two sons in such a dramatic, beautiful and moving way that I wasn't in the slightest bit embarrassed that I had mixed their two names up. He showed me how the Messiah will be like Abel in ways that I would never have been able to work out for myself. His presence was like having an angel of God amongst us. Even David sat before him, asking questions about the Law and events from Israel's history.

Throughout this time, Saul's pursuit of David continued. The reports of his rulership indicated that he had become more and more desperate – going into violent rages again and again. Shouting and screaming at his men ... and, sometimes at Jonathan, his son. Even though enemy nations swept into Israel from time to time, the Philistines especially, the king refused to be swayed from what seemed to have become his sole mission in life – to kill David. More and more bands of soldiers were sent out. Time and again we received reports of their actions. We heard accounts of locals being bribed or threatened.

It was around this time that David and a number of his men left the land altogether for a few months. He even went to Gath – the very city from which Goliath had come, some years before. After that he lived for a while in a cave in Adullam. He managed to rescue his parents from Bethlehem and arranged for them to live in the land of Moab. I know that this caused him great sorrow. He knew that Israel was God's land, and he wanted his parents to be able to live there, surrounded by their friends and family members and, most importantly, by the things of the truth. But he could see that, with Saul acting the way he was, there was no way he could guarantee their safety if they remained in Bethlehem. And living in a tent would have been too hard for Jesse, who was, by now, well over ninety years old!

As the number of men in the Kahal had grown to over four hundred, it became necessary to split into smaller groups. The elders dictated who should move and who should stay, based either on family allegiances or on individual ability.

A number of David's most capable warriors were chosen to remain with him throughout this time, moving on from place to place. He gave these men a title: his "Gibbor" (or "mighty men"). Men like Joab, his two brothers, and Uriah were chosen immediately. I was amazed when the call came for me to join him as well. It was, unquestionably, one of the proudest moments in my life!

We assembled with David in a forest known as Hareth. By this stage a prophet called Gad accompanied David on most of his travels. He was the one who had advised him to leave Gath and return to the land of Judah. While we were in the forest, one young man came to us. He dropped to his knees before David, crying uncontrollably. He wore a linen ephod – the clothing of a priest.

"My lord David", he cried, "the priests, the priests of Nob – they're all dead. Every single one of them has been killed."

"How do you know this?" asked David.

"I was there. I saw it happen. I could do nothing to help. Oh, my lord, what will become of the priesthood now?"

The man's name was Abiathar. Once he had composed himself, he relayed the events of the previous day to us.

King Saul had heard a report that the priests had helped David, and had travelled to Nob to interrogate them. He had a number of his most trusted men with him. When Abimelech (who was the priest who had given bread and the sword of Goliath to David) was asked about this, he claimed innocence. David was the king's son-in-law, he said – why should there be anything wrong in offering aid to such a man?

When Saul heard this, he went berserk. He claimed that everyone in Israel was against him, and that every single priest had to die because of the help that had been given to David. He turned to his soldiers and commanded them to kill the priests. However, they refused. They regarded them as God's servants and were afraid to raise a hand against such men.

Saul was now truly desperate. Once again, he ranted and raged, stating that even his own men were traitors. At this point Doeg the Edomite stepped forward. He had been at Nob when David had met the priests, and he was the one who had reported such things to Saul. The king instructed Doeg to kill the priests – which he did. But he went further. He killed every single person in the city: men, women, children ... even all of the animals.

"How many priests are dead?" asked David.

"Eighty-five, my lord, I'm the only survivor."

"I knew it! I just knew it!" cried Joab. "Didn't I ask for permission to deal with Doeg? Didn't I say he would tell Saul that he'd seen us there? The snake. If he was here today I would take the greatest of pleasure in ..."

"That's enough, Joab", said David. "Nothing we say or do now will bring the priests back. I am, in part, responsible for what happened to them, and I will have to live with this on my conscience forever."

He turned to Abiathar.

"My son, you must remain with us now. Saul wants us dead – and if he knew that there was a witness to his atrocities at Nob, he would want you dead as well. Stay with me and my men. We will protect you. I guarantee that you will be safe with us here in the camp."

After this, we heard that the Philistines had invaded part of the land, and that many of the people from the town of Keilah had been taken captive or were living under Gentile rule. Immediately David asked for guidance from God, and was told to travel to Keilah to save the people.

Within a couple of hours, the entire camp was on the move. We journeyed, as previously, during the evenings or early mornings. If the moon was full we even travelled at night. Within three days we had arrived at Keilah and, even from a distance, could see evidence that the town was in enemy hands. As soon as the men had refreshed themselves and, following a prayer to God, David led us in an assault on the city. What followed was one of the most one-sided battles I've ever been involved in! The enemy soldiers were hopelessly unprepared. I think they had concluded that, as Keilah was only a little town, no Israelite would bother fighting for it. They were wrong.

By the time the night fell, we had taken the entire city. Well over three hundred Philistines were dead; we didn't lose a single man. The enemy soldiers were killed and cast out, their bodies lying in the open fields for the wild animals and birds to devour.

It was during the next few days that the benefit of having a prophet and a priest amongst us became apparent. Some of the people of Keilah had been heard gossiping about David – suggesting that, if the reward was sufficient, they would willingly betray him to Saul. And this after we had risked our lives to rescue them! David asked for guidance from the Lord through the priest, Abiathar. He was told that if we remained in the city, Saul would come down and the people would betray us to him. The time had come to move on again.

We relocated to a wilderness in a district known as Ziph. Living in a desert area is really tough. We were reminded of the time when the nation of Israel had left Egypt and journeyed through the wilderness for forty years, heading towards the Promised Land. These were hard times for us. There were, however, advantages – it's easier to spot someone approaching you in the wilderness than in a forest. And, probably because of the practicalities of sustaining life in such a place, Saul appeared to be reluctant to pursue us there. One man, however, did seek us out. It was Saul's son, Jonathan.

I will never forget the unity which Jonathan and David shared. Their love was special. Really special. They spoke for hours – Jonathan encouraging my lord, telling him to keep going, and assuring him that he would be king one day. David asked about Jonathan's family and friends. He wanted to know about Michal, Jonathan's sister. She was David's wife, but he hadn't seen her for many months. Finally, they renewed their covenant of love, in the presence of the prophet Gad.

Up until that day I never really knew why people spoke so highly of Jonathan. I had heard all about his faith, and how he was a good friend to David – but so were many others. Well, that day I was able to witness first-hand what a great man he was. Others would have complained that the position as "heir apparent" had been lost to them. They would have gone on and on about the unfairness of it all. But not Jonathan. It wasn't that he was unambitious, or a fool. He simply knew that it was God's will that David should reign as the next king and accepted this without a word of complaint. I could see that the character of my lord had been influenced greatly by his friendship with this astonishing man.

A few weeks after this time, history repeated itself. We were living in a wooded area of Ziph known as Hachilah. The men of Ziph made contact with Saul, telling him that we were there. Unsurprisingly, he wasted no time in mustering his troops and coming after us. I'd rarely seen David in such a state of mental anguish. He wasn't afraid for himself. He knew that he would reign as the next king and so, despite Saul's best efforts, he would not be killed. But he was afraid for us. He was like a shepherd, seeking to protect his flock.

We fled from the wood and arrived at another area of desert called Maon. Saul refused to give up. Even from a distance we could see the king's men – a massive number of them – making their way towards us. We were trapped. We climbed part of the way up one of the mountains and prepared for the inevitable attack. David, predictably, stationed himself in front of us. He marshalled his troops, putting us in groups based on experience, ability, and how well we were equipped. Saul's men were so close that we could hear them on the other side of the very mountain where we were hiding. We waited, knowing that, very soon, we would have to fight for our lives.

After about half an hour, David sent Asahel to check and see what was happening. Almost immediately, he was back. Incredibly, the army had retreated – every single man was heading back at a frantic pace. Only afterwards did we learn why: news had reached Saul that the Philistines had invaded the land, and all the fighting men were needed to repel the enemy's advances. As David rightly said, God's timing was impeccable! He knelt before us all, and said we should pray. It was then that he turned to me:

"Hez, would you please lead us in a prayer to our Heavenly Father?"

I was stunned. At first, I didn't know what to say. I had given a few short prayers in front of small numbers of people before – thanks for food and, on one occasion, I had offered some words at the conclusion of the day – but this was something else! Then I looked up and saw Uriah. He was smiling. He clearly thought I could do this, as did David. I took a massive, deep breath, and offered a short, silent prayer first, asking that my nerves wouldn't get the better of me. Although I have little recollection of what I actually said, I know from the booming "Amens" at the end that it was well received.

"Beautiful, Hez", said David, hugging me. "Absolutely perfect."

Obviously, as Saul knew where we were, we couldn't stay at Maon. Within hours we had moved on yet again, arriving at another area of wilderness known as Engedi. We took refuge in the numerous caves there – some of them were large enough to hold around a hundred men at a time.

About a week after this, I was with David and another ten men, when we heard the sound of what we believed to be a battalion of Saul's soldiers getting closer. We nipped into the nearest cave and waited for them to pass. And then the most amazing thing happened. King Saul himself appeared at the mouth of the cave! We heard him speaking to his army commander, Abner. He said that he needed to rest and that the men should scour the nearby caves, in case David was around. Little did he know, but David was in the very cave into which he had entered! What happened next was even more unbelievable. He walked a few feet into the cave, then lay down and went to sleep.

A number of David's men saw this as a chance which was too good to be missed.

"This is your opportunity, my lord ... time to be rid of King Saul for good ... this is the day that God said would come ... He has delivered your enemy into your hand."

David stepped forward. I wasn't sure what he would do. He paused for a couple of seconds, then he took the sword of Goliath and, quickly and quietly, cut off the corner of Saul's robe.

After a while Saul awoke, and he and his men moved on. We were extremely relieved that we had not been discovered, but I could tell that something was wrong. David looked troubled. He looked ill.

"My lord, what's the matter?" I asked.

"I have lifted up my hand against my master", he said. "He is the anointed of Yahweh. I promised that I would never hurt him in any way. To defile the royal garment is a massive thing. I should never, never have done this."

Saul walked a few feet into the cave, then lay down and went to sleep

When Saul and his men were on the other side of the valley, we left the cave and David called after him,

"My lord, King Saul. Why do you chase me, day after day? Why do you listen to lies about me? I don't wish you any ill. Oh my lord, look at your robe. I was in the same cave as you, and could easily have killed you. Some wanted me to spill your blood. But I would not. You are God's anointed. He will judge between us ... but I know, in my heart, that I have protected you today."

We watched as Saul dropped to his knees. Although he was some distance away, we could hear his voice as he sobbed uncontrollably, unable at first to get any words out. Eventually he composed himself.

"My son, David, what a man you are. You are far, far more faithful and kind than I am. I know I have acted shamefully towards you – and yet your actions towards me have been faithful and true. If a man has the chance to kill his enemy, will he let him get away? Well ... you did exactly this today. I know you will be king one day and that this is decreed by God. Now ... when this happens, please will you swear to me that you will not kill my family members?"

In the normal course of events, this is something that no potential king would ever promise. We all knew this. As soon as a member of any new royal house comes to power, one of his (or her) first duties is to remove every trace of the family of those who had gone before. It had certainly happened in other lands. But David was different. His voice rang out across the valley, full of faith and goodness,

"My lord, I vow before you now in the presence of Almighty God that I will do everything I can to protect your family."

Once again, we had all seen the awesome character of David. A mighty man is not simply one who is able to fight and kill. A true warrior for God must be willing to obey His laws – even when those laws demand something which the man would rather not do. Our lord showed us all that his words about not grasping after the kingdom were not idle tales – he really meant this.

The kingdom would certainly be his, at some point in the future. And when that time came, we would be able to share glory at his side, by grace. And that meant waiting patiently for the plan and purpose of God to reach its fruition. As we watched Saul and his army retreating into the distance, none of us knew when that would be, or what we would have to go through first. But we were all certain of one key thing – it would definitely come, one day.

Chapter 10

Samuel's death, Abigail's salvation

SHORTLY AFTER this time, some news reached David which caused him great sorrow. I'd seen him sad before – when Jonathan had left him, for example, or when his parents were taken to live in Moab. But when he heard that Samuel was nearing the end of his life, David was really low. I know he would have wanted to visit him – to have received just a few final words of encouragement and love. And yet, it wasn't to be. Saul's men were stationed all round Ramah. There was no way through.

Within a couple of days the news reached us. The great seer, who had been Israel's guide and leader for so very long, had died peacefully in his sleep. A sense of gloom hung over the Gibbor. Even Joab, who seemed to be untouched by the sorrows of this age, was down. We could all see what this meant – not so much for us, but for Israel as a whole. We had men like Ahithophel and David to teach us. The rest of the nation had Saul – and his spineless, godless, false prophets, who told him what he wanted to hear but rarely, if ever, what the Word of

God actually said. We all knew that, until our lord was installed as king, there would be very little true spiritual guidance in Israel.

Around this time a number of David's men had been stationed near my home town, Carmel. There had been reports of enemy invaders encroaching into Israel from the south. Edomites mostly. But some had come from even further afield – Cushites and Arabians. Animals had been stolen and supplies plundered. David knew how hard this would have hit the poorest in Carmel and the surrounding villages and so decided that a hundred of our men should relocate to the fields outside the city. These soldiers were under the guidance of a great man called Benaiah. He was so valiant in battle that even Joab seemed to be impressed by his exploits.

Times were tough in our camp. We had very little spare food, and some of the men even spoke of returning to their home cities to seek employment there. We had to obtain supplies from any source – and that meant, at times, asking for help from those who could afford it. We never stole or threatened anyone. But when it was clear that it could be afforded, we would ask for anything that could be spared. Most were willing to give us a few loaves or some fruit; maybe even some wine. Occasionally we were told, in no uncertain terms, to clear off. When this happened, we normally walked away. We certainly weren't in the habit of forcing people to part with what they owned. David would even laugh off such acts, saying how different it will be when the Messiah is here and there will be enough for all. But on one key occasion, he didn't do this. And the man who had provoked him was someone I knew very well. It was Nabal of Carmel, the man I had worked for the summer before leaving home.

Why was it that David acted as he did? Why couldn't he just ignore this pathetic fool of a man? I think there were two reasons.

Firstly, Samuel's death had hit him hard. Harder than any of us realised at the time. For a few months he was really down. Grief is a strange thing. It affects people in different ways. And the grief at losing Samuel seemed to make David less reasonable – at least, for a while.

And secondly, David's men had risked their lives to protect Nabal's property and animals for many months. They had seen off numerous attempted raids by Gentile groups and protected the flocks from wild animals, even taking time to repair some of the sheepfolds and storehouses which had been damaged. So when Nabal was asked to spare a few items, we thought he would be only too willing to help. But he refused to do so. He even sent a message back to David, cursing him and accusing him of bringing trouble upon the land of Israel. What a stupid man Nabal was! It was then that David snapped,

"He said what?" he asked.

I was standing a few yards away from Benaiah as he relayed Nabal's response to our lord.

"He said that he sees no reason why he should give his food and drink to anyone like you. He's worked for these things; he should enjoy them."

"Is that it?" asked David. I could sense the tension.

"Well ... not quite. He also said that he's never heard of you or your family. He said there are lots of disobedient slaves in Israel like you who have fled from their masters, and such men should not be encouraged or rewarded."

David let out a cry of anguish which stopped all the members of the Gibbor in their tracks. We all turned to him.

"Into line, mighty men", he demanded. "Weapons on. Now!"

In about 90 seconds we had assembled before him. We lined up in ranks, as an army awaiting their commander's instructions. By now I was starting to get seriously worried. Carmel was my home town and there were many there who I knew well. What was David going to do?

"A man by the name of Nabal has insulted me, my family and all that I hold dear", he informed us all.

"I cannot allow such a slur to go unchecked. As you know, some of our men cared for his flocks and herds for many weeks. They were like a wall of protection, fending off numerous attempts by Gentile enemies to steal food and animals. And although Nabal has plenty that he could give us, he's refusing to help. However he has not simply insulted me. He has insulted the entire group and our way of life. So, we march for Carmel immediately to destroy every male in this man's household."

A cry of agreement went up amongst the group. And yet I was absolutely horrified! I knew many of Nabal's men. I had worked with them for a whole summer. They were, for the most part, decent, honest, hard-working Israelites – many of them with wives and children. Where would this leave these people? I had to appeal to David and beg him to reconsider.

"My lord David", I said, "please hear me out. Please don't do this. I know I have no right to question your authority, but ..."

"You're right, Hez, you haven't. Now, get into line and follow me."

By then he had turned away and was making final preparations for the assault.

"Four hundred men with me and Benaiah", he cried. "Two hundred remain here with Asahel."

I stood rooted to the spot. This was wrong. So wrong. Why punish the men of Nabal's house for their master's stupidity? What about my friends who worked for him? What about his wife, Abigail?

"On the move, Hez. Unless you've lost your nerve?"

I turned round and saw Joab waiting for me to take my place in the line of soldiers.

"Joab, this can't happen", I said. "There are innocent women and children who will suffer. Nabal is a fool – but please don't let our lord do this!"

Joab turned to the other men of our battalion. His voice took on a sarcastic, mocking tone,

"Sounds like we've got a coward in our ranks, men", he remarked, a vile grin on his face. "Our lord demands obedience but this Carmelite here ... well, he wants to pick and choose when to obey. Maybe he's turning traitor?"

I don't know what would have happened if Uriah hadn't stepped in. I suspect I would have gone for Joab – and that would simply have confirmed his opinion that I was disloyal. More than that he would almost certainly have beaten me in the fight, and I would have ended up either shamed, injured or dead.

"Let it go, Hez", said Uriah, dragging me off to the back of the line of soldiers, as far away from Joab as possible. "Our lord has made his decision, and you just have to accept it. If it's not meant to be, our God will spare the people of Carmel. Make it a matter of prayer. Come on – do the right thing."

For the next few hours I prayed like never before. I pleaded, time and time again, that something would happen to make David see sense. Something – anything. A change in the weather? An earthquake? The arrival of some men from Saul's army? I wanted the people of Carmel to be given what I had – the chance to see David as a loving, faithful, forgiving man, not some angry tyrant who took out his frustrations on anyone in his way.

We were about two miles out of Carmel and had just come over the top of a hill when I saw a figure riding towards us. Whoever it was had come alone, but there were other beasts as well – and they seemed to be laden with various items. I managed to fight my way to the front of the group – and straight away I knew who it was. Abigail, looking more beautiful than ever, got down from her ass and bowed herself to the ground before David.

"My lord, please, let me say a few words. You are as an angel of God and know so much. I know that my husband

Abigail, looking more beautiful than ever, got down from her ass and bowed herself to the ground before David

has acted badly towards you. Truly he is such a fool. But please, don't punish others for his sin. If only I had seen your servants when they came, they could have had as much food as they wanted. Please take these provisions which I have brought. If anyone has to be punished, then let it be me. But if you destroy all of Nabal's house ... well, one day, when you have been made king of this great land, it will come back to haunt you."

It was then that I saw the true character of David. Some would have refused to accept Abigail's words. Joab was, I know, absolutely desperate to shed blood that day. But not my lord. David was willing to be swayed.

"I thank my God for sending you today", he said, taking Abigail by the hand and lifting her to stand before him.

"May you be blessed for your bravery and goodness. I promise you that not one of your household will die. I give you my word before Almighty God."

I sank to my knees in prayer. I was so very thankful – this was more than I could ever have asked. Just when I thought there was no way back, our God had intervened, and in a most surprising way.

It was then that I heard a voice behind me,

"Maybe I was right about you, Carmelite. Maybe you are a coward. I mean ... you got your wish after all." It was Joab, and his face bore that same hideous smirk.

"My wish, Joab, was that innocent men and women should not die for the sins of their moronic master. Sorry if that's too hard for you to get your head round."

I could tell that Joab was about ready to attack me ... but, thankfully, David had commanded us to retreat, and he had to obey. I didn't know whether Joab would try to punish me later. To be honest, I didn't care. The people of Carmel were safe. Abigail was safe. That was all that mattered to me at that moment.

Within two weeks we heard that Nabal had died of a massive heart attack. But ... what about his household? What about Abigail? It was then that David called for me to appear before him in his tent.

"Hez", he said, "I owe you an apology. You were right, and I was wrong. There is no way I should have acted as I did when Nabal refused our request for help. You knew that innocent people would suffer, but I wouldn't listen. If it hadn't been for the intervention of that astonishing woman of faith, I might have acted in a way that would have blighted my life forever."

"My lord", I replied, "I'm just thankful that things worked out as they did."

He hugged me.

"Well done, Hez", he said. "Anyone can oppose his enemies. It takes a great man to stand up to his friends. Now, I have a favour to ask of you. Abigail is a widow. I would be honoured if she would agree to be my wife. You know the area well. You know where she lives. Will you travel to see her and ask if she will accept my offer of marriage?"

This was the best part yet! I happily agreed to travel back to Carmel – and, as I suspected would be the case,

Abigail was delighted to accept David's proposal. I would have loved to visit others in my home town at that time, but David had insisted that I come straight back to the camp.

"Saul's men are everywhere", he explained. "And if they hear you've been to Carmel, the people of that place might suffer because of it."

Within the week Abigail and a number of her closest servants had arrived at the camp. In a declaration which was in every way typical of her, she stated that even washing the feet of David's servants would be a position of genuine honour.

Once more, I had seen the hand of our loving Heavenly Father at work in my life and the lives of those around me. It made me realise how powerful Israel's God is. It reminded me of something which I had heard Ahithophel say on a number of occasions: nothing is too hard for the Almighty. Things which may appear hopelessly impossible from man's point of view are possible for Him. He gives, and He takes away. He kills, and He makes alive. And He calls men and women to serve and follow Him.

Chapter 11

Fugitives, part two

I DON'T know why, but after the death of Samuel I had, perhaps subconsciously, concluded that a new age was about to dawn in Israel. I imagined that Saul would die, David would become king and the whole nation would bow before him, acknowledging his greatness. Well, it wasn't quite like that. For the next few years we had to go on living as refugees, hiding out in caves and dens, sometimes sleeping in the open, waiting for the plan and purpose of God to be fulfilled. And all the time we had the sceptre of Saul hanging over us. There was nothing he wouldn't do in his efforts to capture David. And as we were his allies, we were wanted men too.

It was around this time that I heard some news from Carmel which left me surprised, impressed and terrified in equal measure! Saul's men had been in the town, asking after me. They had barged their way into Uncle Jed's house, demanding to know when he and Aunty Jem had last seen me. From the reports that I heard, Uncle Jed was drunk, unable to say what he did the day before, let alone when he last saw his outlaw nephew. Aunty Jemima had simply told them the truth: that she hadn't seen me for over five years, and she had no idea where I was. I wondered how she was; whether she was well, and if she still believed that there was good in me. I longed to see her, to reassure her that I wasn't a criminal – that I had, as she had predicted, come to accept the existence of Almighty God, and was trying to glorify Him in my life. But trying to get to Carmel would have been far too dangerous. For now, I couldn't go anywhere near my home town.

Throughout these hard times, we had to keep on the move. Although some of the locations where we stayed were (relatively) comfortable – dry, large enough and apparently safe – Saul had men in every major town and city. If we stopped too long in any one place and the locals got to know about it, there was every likelihood we would be betrayed. And I think we all knew what that meant. If we were captured, we would be tortured until we told them what we knew. After that, almost certainly, we would be executed as enemies of the Crown.

About two years after we had been to the woods in Hachilah, we headed back there again. We knew that the men of the area had betrayed us to Saul before, but we needed somewhere to go – and perhaps had concluded that the Ziphites would not give us up a second time. We were wrong. Within days of our arrival, Saul led a mini-army of three thousand of his most capable warriors into the area with the intention of tracking us down. One night, David decided that he would head down to the outermost part of Saul's camp. It was, of course, incredibly dangerous. But if we had stayed where we were, they would probably have captured us in a matter of days. We needed to know what Saul had planned. It's possible that David intended to capture one of his men to extract some information. He would never have killed or tortured the man. But we had to know what to do next.

Only six men went down: David, Joab, Abishai, Benaiah, Uriah and me. The others remained at the campsite, with the strict instruction to be ready to fight, or move on, at David's word. When we reached the camp, we knew immediately that something was wrong. Or perhaps more correctly, we knew that something very strange had happened. Fires were burning, and beasts were tied up. But there were no soldiers on guard. Not a single one. David asked me to make my way to the nearest tent and see what I could find out. The others were also dispatched to check tents in different parts of the camp. Silently, and with a degree of trepidation, I crept towards the tent which was about fifty feet away from where we had stopped. One man was lying outside. Initially, I was adamant that it had to be a trap. I made the sound of an owl. No reaction. I coughed. Again, absolutely no response.

I moved closer, all the time suspecting that soldiers would appear at any second. I had my hand on my sword, ready to use it if necessary. When I reached the man, I expected to find him dead. But he was very much alive – just asleep. I nudged his leg – and still he didn't come round. I gave him a shake; still nothing. I opened the flap of the tent and was astonished by the sight that greeted me. Eight men – and all of them asleep. I made my way back to David. By now the other spies had also returned.

"Let me guess", said David, "asleep? Everyone single one of them out cold?"

"Exactly. I wondered if they had been drinking, but that doesn't seem to be the case. And ... well ... the whole army wouldn't be drunk. Not this drunk, anyway."

"Men, there are two possibilities here", said David. "Either it is a trap, and if we make our way towards the centre of the camp, they will wake up and capture us. Or they really are in some sort of deep sleep, and we can do almost anything here."

"My lord", said Uriah, "why not pray and draw lots? Lots have been used in the past in Israel. Ahithophel has told me that there are two stones in the breastplate of the high priest which allow an answer to be given – one of them means yes, the other means no. If we ask for guidance, we will know what we're meant to do."

Joab snorted. He didn't need to say anything. We all knew what he was thinking. Thankfully, David was a man of implicit faith, and saw this as an opportunity which was too good to be missed. He found two small stones: one black, one white, and placed them in a leather pouch. He prayed to God, asking that, if we were to go on, the white stone would be chosen. He then handed me the bag.

"Pick a stone out, please, Hez. If it's the white one, we continue into the camp."

I was suddenly conscious of the potential danger which lay ahead, but like Uriah and my lord, believed that God was guiding us, through His mighty angels. The stone was white.

"Men, this deep sleep is sent from God. He has done this before – specifically when Eve was created from Adam's side. We must go forward in faith. But only one man can accompany me. I refuse to risk the lives of all of you. Now, who will it be?"

Immediately, Abishai asked to go with David, and they went forward towards the centre of the camp. The whole area was eerily silent. We waited, hoping and praying that our lord would be preserved, but not quite sure what would happen next. Would these sleeping men wake up? Would we be captured? Would we have to fight for our lives? And most importantly, what would happen to David?

After about an hour David and Abishai came back. Nothing was said, but they carried with them two items: a spear and a water jar. We made our way back towards our camp, David leading, with Abishai and Joab at the rear. We had been travelling for about a quarter of an hour when I heard Joab ask his brother what had happened.

"Exactly the same as last time. Saul lay asleep. Abner was there as well. Soldiers everywhere. All of them sleeping. I asked for the opportunity to kill Saul. As I said at the time – one strike is all I would need, and we'd be free of him forever. I wouldn't have needed a second chance."

"And ...?" asked Joab.

"He wouldn't let me", replied Abishai. "He said that he's not permitted to touch Saul because he's the anointed king of the land."

"Just like before, then! Honestly, I don't know why we bother!"

I could sense the anger – the complete and utter exasperation – in Joab's voice. He continued his tirade,

"Who knows when we'll be free? Saul could live for another twenty years, and we'd still be living out in the open, being chased from one place to the next. If you ask me, David's lost it ..."

Up until then, I had kept my emotions in check. But that last comment was too much. I rounded on Joab, grabbed him and threw him to the ground. I knelt over him and pushed my face close to his. For the first time ever, I sensed fear in those cold, grey eyes.

"Don't you ever say a word against my lord in my hearing again!" I yelled. "Do you hear me?"

It was then that Benaiah grabbed me and hauled me off. As I looked round, I saw that Abishai was helping Joab up. He looked as if he'd just had the biggest fright of his life.

"What on earth's going on here?" asked Uriah.

"Nothing I can't handle", I snapped. "Come on, let's go."

We made our way back to the camp in complete silence. I knew what Joab was like. He never forgot, and it wasn't in his nature to forgive. One day, I suspected,

I rounded on Joab, grabbed him and threw him to the ground

he would exact his revenge. But I had taken his snide remarks about others for long enough. I didn't care what he said about me; I wouldn't allow him to insult my lord and saviour.

As soon as the sun was up we positioned ourselves on the side of a valley where we could see Saul's tent. David called to him and his men, as before,

"Abner, servant of King Saul, can you hear me? I came into the camp last night and could have killed you all."

"Who is this that dares to cry to the king?" asked Abner.

"My lord, King Saul, this is your servant and spiritual son, David. I have here your spear and water jar. I stood over you last night and could have taken your life. I was merciful to you. Why do you chase me? Why do you hate me so much?"

As before, Saul was full of remorse. He sounded genuine. But then again, he had sounded genuine the last time.

"I have sinned, my son, I have sinned", he cried. "I gave you my word that I would not pursue you, and I went back on my vow. I am so sorry. I promise before these witnesses that I will leave you in peace from now onwards. You will be king after me. I know that now. And I know you will achieve great things on the throne of Israel."

I looked round at Joab, daring him to comment. For once, he was silent. I was thankful at least for that. Maybe my threats of the previous evening had done some good?

After a lad from Saul's camp had come to retrieve the two items, we stood and watched the king and his men as they packed up their belongings and headed back the way they had come. We all hoped that this would be the start of a time of peace within the camp – that we would be able to remain in the same place for more than a day or two. Or perhaps we would be able to return to the Kahal and live there. Well, what happened next took us all by surprise. David called us all to him the following day,

"My mighty men, I thank you, as always, for your loyalty to me. I will never forget it. And I thank our gracious Heavenly Father for His goodness in bringing every one of you here. Now ... as you know, Saul has vowed that he will not pursue us any more. But I don't know if we can trust him to keep his word. He's promised this before. I imagine that he will keep chasing us, and I refuse to allow your lives to be endangered because of your allegiance to me. So, we move on tonight and will seek sanctuary over the Philistine border, at least for a time. There's no way that Saul will follow us there."

We were all amazed by this. No man was more passionate about the things of Israel than David. No man loved the land and the Law more than he did. He was always talking about the city in the heart of the land – Jebus – and how it would be taken by Israelites again one day. And into Philistia ... he was hardly the most popular man there! We'd all heard the songs that the women of the land used to sing:

"Saul has killed his thousands, but David his ten-thousands."

This didn't refer to actual numbers of men killed. This described David's victory over Goliath – a man who was worth so many more than the average foot soldier. And Goliath was a Philistine. He was their champion. Their national hero. So, heading into Philistine territory was, to say the least, a little strange. What followed was stranger still: we ended up in Gath – the very home city of Goliath!

We stayed in and around that place for the next few months. News reached us that Saul had proclaimed to his men that he would not pursue us now that we had left the land. So, maybe we were right to have departed from Israel? David's wives were with us, and his children. Some of the other men also had their families alongside them. And even though (amazingly!) the people of Gath were reasonably hospitable, the city was unable to support such a massive number of newcomers. I was with David when he met the King of Gath, a man called Achish, one day.

"My lord", said David, "you have been good to me and my men since we arrived here. We are very thankful for that."

"David, you have brought peace to our region. There have been no invasions by Israelites since your arrival. And your men have done much work here – building and repairing houses and parts of the city walls."

"Thank you my lord. And yet ... we can't continue living here. The city just won't support so many people."

"Well, if you must move on, I understand", replied Achish. "There is a deserted town not far from here which you could use. In fact, it was once part of Israel. The name is Ziklag."

Ziklag: we all knew about that place. It was in the area originally allotted to the tribe of Simeon, but had been captured by the Philistines and then left desolate. Hardly anybody lived there now. An empty, hollow shell. When I was a lad, "Ziklag" was a phrase used for somewhere that was particularly cold and soulless. But ... at least it would be home, and it would be within the area of land originally given to Israel. And if Saul regarded it as beyond the Philistine border, perhaps we might find safety at last?

Within the week, we were on the move yet again. Our time in Gath had been weird! We had received more courtesy in this Gentile city than in many places in Israel. But we could never stay there for long. For our lord, the call of home grew stronger every day. He longed to be back in God's land. So, with David and his family at the head, and his men, with their wives, children and animals all following – a mini exodus, really – we made our way back towards the land originally promised to Abraham, with the barren town of Ziklag before us. We hoped and prayed that we would find some comfort and peace there.

Chapter 12

A home ... of sorts

IN MY day, there were a number of beautiful locations in Israel. Tirzah, for example, was a few miles north of Shechem. What a place! And Jebus – despite the fact it was still in the hands of Gentiles – was also wonderful to behold. As a city set on a hill, it shone at night like a beacon in the darkness. So yes, there were plenty of beautiful sites in the land. And then ... there were places like Ziklag.

When we arrived, we found it virtually deserted. A few poverty-stricken Philistine families, scratching out a living in any way they could, but nothing more. David kindly offered them the opportunity to remain in their homes – but stressed that they would have to abide by our standards if they chose to stay.

The majority of the city was a complete mess – walls broken down, gates burnt to a cinder, rubble strewn everywhere, piles of rubbish left in the streets. The whole place stank like a sewer. Not wishing to appear ungrateful, I could see why the Philistines were so willing to hand it over to us! But at least we had a home. And as we were 'officially' over the border in Philistia, it seemed unlikely that Saul would lead an army against us.

The first few months were spent making the city fit for human habitation. Once again I found that my skills as a carpenter were in great demand. David put me in charge of making and repairing anything made of wood: doors, gates, beams, window frames and furniture. I was able to choose a team of men to work with me. We began by deciding which items could be restored – so much was damaged beyond repair and had to be burned. Once the necessary repairs were completed, we set about making the new stuff. Thankfully there were plenty of trees growing nearby: sycamore and acacia, mostly. Although we had a fairly poor selection of tools, we were able to fell a number of trees and the wood was used to make all sorts of items for the city.

All around us, men worked on the houses and the city wall. To his credit, Joab was a very hard worker and extremely capable in building and repairing walls. We never spoke, however. After that last incident we just avoided each other altogether.

In a few weeks, the transformation at Ziklag was amazing. With God's blessing, and through an enormous amount of hard work, it looked more like a city and less like a building site.

Unlikely as this may sound, a number of Philistines had chosen to come with us from Gath. They were known as Gittites. They had been so impressed by our lord during his time there that they had decided to follow him when he left their home city. Some of our men were clearly not happy about this. They didn't voice their objections openly, but it was obvious that they weren't impressed. I couldn't understand this mindset at all! One of the greatest men in the camp – a fantastic friend, a mighty warrior and a spiritual giant – was Uriah. And he was a Hittite by birth. Why would we turn away people who wanted to learn about Israel's God and serve our lord?

We had been in Ziklag for around a year when enemy nations started sending parties of men, raiding our supplies and stealing animals. They came up from the south, and when this happened the third time, David decided to act. He assembled all the fighting men, and we invaded the area of land between the south-west of Israel and the border of Egypt. We destroyed great numbers of men: Geshurites, Gezrites and also a number of Amalekites. Some of these were probably descendants of the very people Saul had refused to kill all those years before.

We retrieved many of the beasts that had been stolen, but were able to take so much more – weapons, clothes, tools, food and animals. That was the end of the raiding parties from the south. No other Gentile groups oppressed us after that.

A few months after this, something happened which I know caused a lot of confusion for many – both in our group, and in the rest of Israel. Achish, King of Gath, had met with David regularly during this time. He was astonished by the transformation in Ziklag. I think he and the rest of the Philistines had concluded that it would lie desolate forever. It was around this time that he voiced his opinion that our lord would never return to live in Israel – that he had "turned Philistine". We all knew better. David was more focused on the Hope of Israel than ever before. He sat before Ahithophel three or four times a week to be instructed in the word. I was with him on many of these occasions, and was stunned by his faith and love for the law. He wrote a number of psalms which we sang. Many of these would go on to be known and loved throughout Israel in the following years.

During one of his visits, I overheard Achish talking with my lord about a forthcoming battle. As one of David's key men, I was permitted to be part of these discussions.

"David, my son, you've transformed this place", said Achish, "I wouldn't have believed it was possible in such a short time."

"Thank you, my lord. We've been greatly blessed. And we are thankful to you for allowing us to have this city."

The two men hugged. Achish went on,

"Now, as you know, there are enemies of the Philistines everywhere. It seems likely that we will be at war with Israel once again. Saul is amassing troops near our border. I need to know if I can count on your support."

"I will fight against the enemies of my lord, whoever they may be", replied David.

We didn't quite know what to make of this – but we knew better than to question David's judgment. I had done so in the matter regarding Nabal, but this was different. Within two weeks, the Gibbor were marching in line behind our lord, set to join the Philistine army at Aphek. We were (apparently) all ready to go out with them when one of the lords of the Philistines raised his concerns. He was adamant that David would turn against Achish when the battle began and would side with Israel. As a result of this, we were not allowed to take part in that conflict, and made our way back towards Ziklag.

I know what was said by some of David's enemies at the time. They even said it afterwards, well into his reign as king on the throne of Israel. They said he was a traitor. That he had "gone native" – that he was now a Philistine in his heart, and had gone back on his promise not to hurt Saul. Well, unlike most of his accusers, I knew the real David. I spent many, many years with the man. I saw him in times of strength and weakness; in times of faith and, occasionally, doubt. But never – EVER – would he have fought against Israel. When he vowed a vow, he kept it. And for him to fight against King Saul – particularly when Jonathan was still alive and was numbered amongst the armies of Israel – was, quite simply, impossible.

So, why did he say he would go out alongside Achish? To be honest, I really don't know. But I rather imagine that the Philistine lord was right all along: David would have taken the opportunity to return to Israel. All I do know – and there can never be any question about this – is that David was one of the most loyal Israelites I've ever met. And fighting alongside Philistines against Israel – regardless of how sinful or wayward Saul was at that time – would never have happened.

The journey back to Ziklag took three days. As we neared the city however, we knew immediately that something was wrong. Seriously wrong. Great plumes of black smoke rose high into the sky. The city gates – which we had taken many hours repairing – were lying flat on the ground, a smouldering ruin. As we arrived at the city walls, we could hear the sounds of women and children crying. We raced inside and found a few small children and one or two women, who had been in hiding. Everyone else was gone.

We waited while the women regained their composure, and then asked what had happened. It turned out that some other Amalekites had attacked the city from the south. A mighty army had amassed around the city walls. Within a matter of hours they had burned down the gates and gained access to the city. They had stolen everything that they could carry – and taken the women and children hostage. Even David's two wives, and his sons and daughters, were gone.

It was then that I heard things which, even to this day, make me shudder. Some men, incredibly, spoke of stoning David. I don't know who they were, and he never tried to find out. To his credit, I think he could see that these were just spur-of-the-moment comments. I suppose we all say and do things we regret in times of great trial or sadness. Throughout this terrible time, David – a man who had lost both of his wives and all of his children – acted with the utmost faith and courage.

When it was established what had actually happened, David asked for guidance from God. He called three men

Great plumes of black smoke rose high into the sky

before him: Ahithophel, his spiritual advisor, Abiathar, the priest, and Gad, the prophet. They sat together, praying and worshipping for about an hour. After this he gathered us together.

"My faithful friends: today has been a dark day for us all. A dark day indeed. But I believe that our gracious Heavenly Father will bless and keep our families, and that they can – and will – be restored to us. Now, I know that you are greatly distressed by the loss of your loved ones. But if you are willing to trust me and follow me now, I am certain that they will be safe. Are you with me, mighty men? Will you follow me now?"

Immediately, Benaiah stepped forward,

"My lord, I am yours. I will remain by your side, wherever you go."

Uriah and I followed. Then, one by one, the rest of the group did the same. In less than an hour, six hundred men were marching south, following the tracks left by the enemy. We hoped and prayed that we would be blessed and that our beloved families would be preserved. I remember asking over and over again for our Father to keep and care for those who had been taken. I wasn't married at the time and didn't have nieces or nephews amongst the group, but was very conscious of the bond of love which existed between husbands and wives, parents and their little ones.

The journey was horrendous. A biting wind brought a constant, driving rain from the direction of the Great Sea. It was bitterly cold, with some sleet. By the time we took refuge in a cave near the brook Besor, some of the men were too tired to go on. David decided that they should remain there, and the rest of us continued the pursuit.

After about another mile, and just when we thought we would have to take shelter for the night, we found a young man lying in a field. He was so tired, thin and cold, we wondered if he was about to die. Thankfully, when he was given something to eat and drink and was warmed by a campfire, he revived a little. He was an Egyptian slave. He had been owned by one of the Amalekite lords who had led the attack on Ziklag. When he had become ill he had been abandoned – just left to die, out in the open. David wanted to know details.

"Where are the Amalekites now? Can you take us to them?"

The man seemed more than a little unsure.

"Well, I know where they'll be ... but I need you to give me your word that I won't be handed over to them. I want you to promise me that I will be safe."

"My son", said David, "I vow before Yahweh, the Mighty One of Israel, that your life will be preserved."

After that he led us right to the camp. They were about five miles away from us. Even before we reached the location, we could hear them singing. Moronic music blared out, announcing their presence to anyone nearby. Many of them were drunk – staggering round in circles or dancing. Others lay on the ground, obviously having consumed so much wine that they were out cold.

We began our attack at twilight. The battle lasted until the evening of the next day. I lost count of the number of men I slaughtered. They were totally unprepared for us – and even those who were able to handle a sword were no match for David's mighty men. A number managed to escape on camels. The rest were, quite simply, butchered. I'd never been involved in a more one-sided contest. Not one member of the Gibbor was lost. Every single woman and child was safe. Even the goods were all retrieved. And we were able to capture lots more – items they had obviously stolen from other cities.

Once we were back in Ziklag, and when the necessary repairs had been made (lots more work for the carpenters!), David sat down with a chosen number of close friends and advisors. I was incredibly honoured to be asked to join him. Benaiah was there, and Uriah. Abishai was invited ... but not Joab. I hadn't said a word to anyone about his comments that night after we had visited Saul's camp. But David knew what was going on. He was so wise. He knew the hearts of all of his men.

"My faithful men ... my Gibbor ... my friends ... well done. Every single member of our family unit has been saved, and we've repaired the city gates and walls."

"And on top of that, we've gained so much more", said Abishai. "Ziklag must be one of the richest cities in the south."

"Yes ... and this is what troubles me. This is why you're here. What strikes you as unusual about the wealth which we took from the Amalekite camp? The clothing especially?"

"It looks familiar", replied Benaiah. "It almost looks as though it was stolen from an Israelite city. The items of clothing have blue borders."

"Exactly", said David. "I spoke to that Egyptian servant boy about the actions of our enemies. It seems that they raided a number of towns in Israel before heading here. Now, I wouldn't feel comfortable keeping all the spoils if I knew that so many of those things had been stolen from cities in God's land."

"So what do you have in mind, my lord?" asked Uriah.

"I believe that we should gather the excess – everything which didn't come from Ziklag originally – and distribute it to the cities which we suspect were raided by the Amalekites. Now ... who's with me in this?"

One by one we indicated our support for the plan. When we spoke to the others about this, some were reluctant to hand over what they had retrieved from the Amalekite camp. And yet, the word of David possessed enormous power. When we explained the reason for our actions, most gave up their spoils without complaint. A few, I suspected, had kept back certain items. Well, that was a matter for them and their consciences. We know what happened to Achan when the nation entered the land. They would have to live with what they had done if others had returned goods and they had refused to do so.

When the spoils were finally gathered together, David made a list of thirteen key areas which he thought may have been raided – or locations where we had been given support over the previous few years. He divided

the items into equal shares, and they were sent to t
places.

Little did we know, but around this very time, Saul was doing battle with the Philistines in Mount Gilboa. It would, in fact, be his last ever conflict. He, three of his sons, and many, many men of Israel lay dead at the end of that terrible day. Jonathan – that great, courageous, loving giant of faith – that mightiest of mighty men – was amongst the dead.

That tragic, awful time would see changes for a large proportion of Israelites. Widows were many in number. Children were fatherless; others were orphaned. Farms and businesses failed altogether because of the number of men who were killed. And for David? Well, that terrible time would prove to be the catalyst for his ultimate elevation to the throne of Israel. So what about his mighty men ... his Gibbor, those who had remained true to him while he fled from Saul? We would enjoy great privileges at his side as he was raised to rule over God's great, glorious land.

Chapter 13

Long live the King!

WE HAD waited for this day for so very, very long. Within the Kahal we had talked about it, prayed about it and occasionally, some of us had even dreamed about it! Well, at long last, the time had come. David was to become king! OK, it was only over part of the land, but at least he was a king. And we all suspected that it would only be a matter of time before he would rule over the whole nation.

News of the death of Saul came to us in a rather unusual way. A man had staggered up to the gates of Ziklag and collapsed on the ground before David. He gave the impression of having been in a battle. After we had given him something to drink, he relayed to us what had happened:

"My lord, I come from the conflict. Bad news I'm afraid. Many from Israel are dead. Saul and Jonathan are amongst the slain."

"How do you know this?" asked David.

Considering he appeared to have been at death's door when he arrived at the city, the man was now miraculously revived. He said he was an Amalekite and had happened to pass by Mount Gilboa, arriving at the site of Israel's final battle with the Philistines. He saw Saul lying on the ground, mortally wounded. The king called out to him, asking him to end his life. He said that the Philistines were getting closer, and that Saul said that he didn't want to be captured and tortured by them.

"So I did the kind thing. I ended the poor man's suffering. I also removed his crown and royal bracelet, and have brought them to you, my lord. Now you can reign as king. The way is open for you."

Initially I wasn't sure how David would react. The man's story sounded far-fetched. How could he have been so close to the king – with the enemy in sight – but then have sufficient time to remove objects of value from him and still be able to escape? When David examined the items in question, there was no doubt about it, they were Saul's. Which meant – regardless of any inaccuracies in the account presented to us by this Amalekite – the king and his son were almost certainly dead.

David dropped to his knees, holding his head in his hands. He remained there for about a minute, and then began to cry. He sobbed and sobbed. His whole body shook. He tore his clothes in anguish. One by one, we followed suit. I didn't really know any of Saul's family well. I'd only ever met Jonathan on a few brief occasions. But I knew what kind of a man he was. And I knew how much this meant to my lord. We fasted for the rest of the day, sitting in silence on the open ground.

As the night fell, the Amalekite was called to stand before David once again.

"I imagine you feel you deserve a reward for removing the man who stood between me and the throne of Israel?"

The man had a look of anticipation on his face. This was, very clearly, what he wanted. His voice took on a tone of fake humility:

"Well ... I simply put a dying man out of his misery, my lord. Should you see fit, in your wondrous generosity, to grant anything to me, I would gladly accept it, although I was simply doing what anyone would ..."

It was then that my lord leapt to his feet.

"Silence, you vile, money-grabbing Amalekite dog! You claim to have killed Saul: the anointed king of Israel, the one chosen and appointed by Almighty God. How dare you do this? And how dare you then come before me, begging for some sort of compensation?"

He turned to one of his youngest followers,

"Kill this evil man now. Get him out of my sight."

The young man obeyed, and we carried the body out of the city and left it for the wild birds to devour.

"Even if he was lying, he brought it on himself", said David. "He claimed to have killed Yahweh's anointed king. No one who lifts up a hand against such a man can remain unpunished."

For the next few hours, David lamented the loss of Saul and his mighty son. He spoke of Saul's courage and strength, and how he had granted great favours to many within the nation. But his words about Jonathan were the most hard-hitting. To this day I've never forgotten them – or the distress in the voice of my lord. He was so grief-stricken, he could barely get the words out,

"Jonathan, my brother, my friend. I've never met anyone like you. Our love was special. Even my wives – those who know me best – aren't as close to me as you were. The mighty have fallen in Israel this day. Great darkness had descended on our land. Truly, the mighty have fallen."

After a brief prayer uttered by Ahithophel, we made our way to our rooms in silence. No singing. No rejoicing. No laughter. Not a single word was spoken. We all knew what this meant for our lord, and we shared his grief that Jonathan was lost. It was one of the saddest times David would ever go through.

Three days later, at the instruction of God, we left Ziklag and headed for a place which I knew very well: Hebron! That journey was, I have to admit, somewhat surreal for me. We sang for joy as we neared the city, praising the Almighty that the time had come for His promises about David to be fulfilled. Nobody was worried about being arrested. For the first time in many years we were free men!

And yet, as we passed through the massive wooden gates leading to the inner part of the city, I have to admit that I felt more than a little uncomfortable. I wasn't concerned about Ben Obal. I imagined he had probably moved on to another city and was busy robbing others there – telling tales about his thriving tannery and his elderly relations. No, my concerns related to those who knew me best in the city: the Boss and Han especially. I had behaved so badly the last time we met, and I knew that I had to make amends for my actions.

Within a couple of hours, David had arranged a meeting with the elders of the city. There were so many of us: six hundred men, plus women, children and animals. There wasn't really enough room for us all. It was therefore decided that David would remain at Hebron with a small number of mighty men, and the others would settle in the towns and villages round around the city. Once this had been agreed, I requested permission to head off to see my former workmates.

As I rounded the corner of the street where I had worked all those years before, my heart started beating faster. Would the workshop still be there? Would the Boss still be in charge? And if so, what would I say to him? Would I be welcomed back? What had he heard about me – did he believe I was a criminal?

I stood at the entry to the shop, not quite knowing what to do next. Five men were working away, and in the corner, in his familiar position, sat the Boss. He hadn't changed a bit. He still had that striking mane of white hair and bushy beard. I coughed, and he looked up. For a few seconds he didn't seem to be able to work out who I was. Then he gave an enormous cry and leapt from his seat, running over to greet me. I'd never seen him run before.

"Hez, my boy! You're alive! Thank God, you're alive!" He lifted me off the ground and held me so tightly that, for a few seconds, I have to confess I had a little difficulty in breathing. There were tears streaming down his face. Of the other men who had been at the workshop all those years before, only two were still there. They were also delighted to see me and came over and hugged me.

"You know", said the Boss, wiping the tears from his lined face, "I thought I would never see you again. If only you knew how many nights I've lain awake, cursing myself for being too hard on you that day. I'm so sorry for the way I acted. I've prayed and prayed that one day you would come back here. Now, at last, I can die a happy man."

At this point I was also overcome with emotion, and we embraced again, both of us sobbing like little children.

"Boss", I said, "I'm the one who should be apologising. I should never have spoken to you the way I did, and I'm truly sorry for the hurt I caused you. I regretted it as soon as I'd said it, but, stupid little kid that I was, I thought I knew best."

After a while we composed ourselves, and sat and chatted. I explained how I had got into trouble gambling and had fled from the city, having been attacked.

"Oh, my son, I wish you had come to me. I would have covered your losses", he said.

"I felt so ashamed." I shook my head and sighed. "The man in question was so friendly early on and I won so much. Then, well ... everything went wrong."

He lifted me off the ground and held me so tightly

"This man ... was he called Ben Obal? Did he say he was from the valley of Sorek?"

"Yes, how did you know?"

"He did the same thing to a few others, and eventually he was found out. One of his victims was beaten to death about two years ago, and Ben Obal was taken and tried by the elders. They found him guilty of murder and he was stoned outside the city walls."

I wasn't greatly surprised, and I certainly didn't feel any sorrow for him. I felt for all those poor souls whose lives had been blighted by his lying words and hateful actions. I was invited to eat with the Boss and Han and, after confirming that this was acceptable with my lord, had a lovely meal with them that evening. We talked and talked until the early hours about David, life in the Kahal, how I had served him as one of the Gibbor, and the times we had avoided Saul's attempts to capture us. The Boss listened, enthralled. He was most interested to hear about the two meetings with Samuel.

"He's the one who told me about David becoming king", he said. "I knew it would happen one day. I just knew it. And to think ... you're one of his mighty men! Oh Hez, what an honour!"

I even slept in my old room that night. It meant so much to be back in a place which was, in many ways, home to me – and to share the company and love of a man who was far, far more than a boss. More like a father, really.

The next day the elders of a number of the major cities and towns of Judah – Lachish, Beersheba, Bethlehem and more – assembled at Hebron. Each had brought a gift for David. In due course they were invited to stand before him.

"My lord David", said the spokesman, "you were always destined to be king one day. We know what you did to the Philistine giant ... but more importantly we also know of the promises made to you by our God through Samuel. We bow before you this day, acknowledging that you are the rightful possessor of the throne of Israel. We are your grateful subjects."

Abiathar the priest then appeared with a ram's horn of oil, and David was anointed as king. He expressed his gratitude to those who had gathered before him and spoke of the honour of becoming ruler over Israel. But he also stressed that no relations of Saul were to be treated badly. He even mentioned the men from the city of Jabesh-Gilead who had risked their lives to retrieve the bodies of Saul and his sons from Philistia. He told us that they should be commended. He didn't want anyone oppressing them because of their allegiance to the former king.

What should have been the commencement of a time of peace and prosperity within the nation was, in fact, the very opposite. Abner, Saul's army commander, took one of the surviving sons of King Saul, a man by the name of Ishbosheth, and made him king over the rest of the land. For the time being at least, David would rule only over Judah.

And so the next couple of years saw a time of great unrest in God's land. Although there was never outright civil war, there were constant skirmishes, notably along the 'border' between Israel and Judah. During one of these occasions, Asahel, the brother of Joab and Abishai, lost his life. I won't go into the precise details of the battle nor will I describe the way he was killed – except to say that the man who took his life did everything to avoid it, and acted wholly acceptably. It is the outcome of these terrible events which will stay with me for ever. Joab and Abishai swore vengeance on the man who was responsible. That man was Abner. I was with Joab and the others as we walked back to Hebron, with two men carrying Asahel's lifeless body behind us.

"My brother, we cannot allow this act of treachery to go unchecked", said Abishai.

"Don't you worry. I will not let that happen." The hatred – the determination to exact what he believed to be appropriate revenge – was very clear in the voice of Joab.

"One day, the murderer of our brother will be made to pay for what he has done. I will shed his blood if it's the last thing I do. The sons of Zeruiah will not be shamed."

Zeruiah was the mother of Joab, Abishai and Asahel – and the sister of David. Although David was the uncle of these men, Zeruiah was one of Jesse's oldest children, and David was the youngest, which made him about the same age as his three nephews. My lord knew the characters of these men better than anyone. And he knew that Joab was a man who did things his own way – regardless of the opinions or feelings of anyone else and no matter what God's law said.

However, after this awful incident, the following few years were, generally speaking, a time of stability in Judah, and also within our group. The mighty men, at the king's instruction, were sent out to the towns and villages over which David ruled. They were "overseers". They weren't meant to take charge in these cities – the elders of those places already did this – but they were required to bear the name of David in these locations and ensure that everything was being done acceptably. They were the king's own personal ambassadors.

Where there were disputes, they would take the matter back to the king for his guidance. They collected taxes and gave guidance to those who, for whatever reason, felt unable to approach the elders of the city in question. They oversaw building projects, ensuring that cities and towns were well fortified. Most importantly they sought to ensure that the rule of law, laid down by David, was understood and obeyed. And that law, of course, was the law of Almighty God, given through Moses.

However, the mighty men were still primarily warriors. They made up David's own personal fighting unit – his closest and most trusted followers. Ten men were stationed at Hebron at any one time as personal guards to our king and his family. When our lord or any of his wives or children went out of the city, they went as well. After three months they would move on, returning to one of the other cities or towns of Judah to take up their positions there. Then others of the Gibbor would assemble to Hebron to guard the king.

When Gentile raiders crossed the borders oppressing people from Judah (or even Israel), David would dispatch a battalion of men, led by three or four of the Gibbor. The resulting conflicts demanded an enormous amount of courage, faith and organisation. We were commanding men who, in some cases, had very little practical experience of warfare. We had to teach them, lead them and protect them. Like David, we were shepherds, and they were our sheep. And yet, with God's blessing, we were able to enjoy great successes, not only over Gentiles but also in taking certain parts of the land of Israel. All the time David's kingdom grew stronger and larger, and the realm of Ishbosheth, weaker and smaller.

One day, to our great surprise, some messengers arrived at Hebron. Nothing unusual there, as all sorts of people came to see our lord throughout this time, except that these men had come from Abner, and carried with them a declaration, stating that he wanted to side with David and would do all that he could to ensure that the whole nation was brought under his rule! David was happy with this; however, he insisted that his wife, Michal, who was Saul's daughter, had to be restored to him. Abner agreed to this request and then went throughout the land of Israel, making the people aware that he believed David to be the chosen king, and that they should unite under his leadership. Well, Abner was clearly a very persuasive man, as they were all in agreement with this.

A few months after this, Abner arrived back at Hebron, along with twenty of his closest and most trusted men. I was stationed at the city at the time and was invited to be part of the discussions which took place between them. This was a pivotal time for the royal houses of Saul and David.

It became apparent that Ishbosheth was a weak man – much more like his father Saul than his great and mighty brother, Jonathan. He would often accuse people of acts of treachery. One day, he had dared to make an accusation – something which was entirely unfounded – against Abner. This was the final straw for this great man. He decided to reject Saul's son, and side with David. Throughout that meeting, Abner's decency and honesty shone through. He wasn't vindictive. It wasn't simply that he had been insulted and was unable to forgive. No, it became clear that he could see that David was the one appointed by God to sit on the throne of Israel, and he wanted to do all that he could to support him in this. A divided nation of Israel was a country in a state of weakness. Under one king, God's people would be far, far stronger.

Well, one man who was normally stationed at Hebron was absent that day: Joab. By the time he returned to the city, an agreement had been made and Abner had been sent away in peace. Unsurprisingly, Joab was seething when he heard this. I was with David when he stormed into the room:

"What have you done? How dare you invite that murderer in here? How on earth can you agree to any sort of league with him? He's the enemy!"

"Joab, I know how you feel", replied David. "But Abner is a decent man and he wants to play his part in bringing the whole of the land under our rule. I believe that he is genuine in this."

"Well I don't!" yelled Joab. "And I refuse to work with you if he's part of our government. You can count me out."

He and Abishai then stormed out of the room. I imagined he was resigning his 'commission' as a mighty man – that he would leave the administration of David and we'd never hear from him again. Well, this wasn't the case. What came next took us all by surprise.

Joab sent a message to Abner, asking him to return to Hebron. And when he did, in an act of immense cowardice, he murdered him. Don't get me wrong; had he challenged Abner to a duel, that would probably have been regarded as acceptable to us all. Chivalrous, even. But we all knew what Joab had done. He pretended to hug Abner and used a hidden dagger to kill him. Joab was, without question, a great and mighty warrior. He had saved David's life on a number of occasions – and for that I was, and always will be, extremely grateful. But that day he was a bigger coward than someone who turns and runs away when he sees an enemy coming. Not one of the Gibbor wanted anything to do with him after that. David was horrified at what he had done. He even walked behind the body of Abner, as he was laid to rest in Hebron, sobbing uncontrollably. He then fasted and mourned for the rest of the day.

"A great man – a mighty and noble prince of Israel is dead today", he cried. "As king of the land, I am in a position of great strength – but I feel weak because of the actions of Zeruiah's sons. I know that our God will deal with these men. They will pay the price for their sins one day."

By now Ishbosheth must have been terrified of David, and extremely apprehensive as to what lay ahead for him. Without Abner's support, there was no way he could have continued as king. One day, as he lay on his bed, two of his servants crept into his chamber and murdered him. They then cut off his head and travelled through the night to appear before David. They were ushered into his room, and presented their grisly trophy before him.

"Our lord, King David", they said, their voices full of self-congratulation. "Now you can reign over the whole land. Your God has removed all your enemies. May all the seed of Saul, the weak and faithless King of Israel, be destroyed, so that your royal house can rule in righteousness forever!"

We all knew what was going on. These men, like that Amalekite a few years before, wanted a reward. They expected David to be pleased with them. In all my years with that great and faithful man, I had rarely seen him as angry.

"Some years ago, a man came to me, claiming to have put Saul out of his misery when he was already dying. On that occasion, he expected me to give him some sort of payment for his actions. I didn't do so. I had him killed for daring to raise a hand against God's anointed king. And you?" He rose from his seat and grabbed one of them by the throat.

"You are far, far worse!" he shouted. "You dare to come in here expecting me to reward you – when you vile, evil cowards have killed a decent man as he slept in his own bed?"

He turned to his youngest bodyguards and instructed them to kill these two traitors. Once they were executed their hands and feet were severed, and they were hung up outside the wall of Hebron for all to see. This is what David thought of these men. Their actions were all wrong. They had been 'heading in the wrong direction'.

If someone who stands between a man and a position of greatness is taken out of the way – then the man in question will normally be extremely glad. Most men, in David's position, would have rejoiced at the events of that particular day. Well, our lord wasn't like most men. And, although the way was now cleared for him to take his place on the throne of Israel, ruling over the whole land, this had come about through evil acts, performed by spineless, vicious, grasping men. David, despite being a mighty warrior-king, was also a man who loved peace and hated violence. And he encouraged those closest to him to do the same.

Chapter 14

Zion, in Israelite hands at last

IT DIDN'T take long for the rest of Israel to catch on. They could see what a brilliant ruler David was, and how the people of Judah had benefited from his wisdom, mercy and love. It was about three months after the death of Ishbosheth when representatives of many of the major cities in the rest of Israel assembled at Hebron, bowing low before our lord.

"We are your bone and your flesh", they declared. "Even in days gone by, when Saul was the figurehead, you possessed the power. We know that it is determined by God that you should reign, and we happily accept you as our divinely-appointed monarch!"

"If this is the case", I thought to myself, "then why didn't you give us more support when Saul was trying to kill us? What about places like Ziph and Keilah, who betrayed us to the king? Where are their elders? Let's hear what they have to say!"

David, wisely, chose not to mention these matters. He believed that everyone deserved a second chance and that, as king over the whole nation, he should commence his reign with the people having 'a clean slate'. So, for the third and final time, David was anointed. A short time prior to his battle with Goliath, Samuel had anointed him, in the presence of his brothers. Later, Abiathar had poured oil on his head when he began to rule over Judah. Now he was anointed again, this time as the king of all Israel. We shouted for joy and sang psalms, glorifying our gracious Heavenly Father and his chosen king. It was one of the happiest days of my entire life.

Now, the first acts of leaders are often of great significance. The people of Israel looked to David at that time wondering what his initial act would be. Would he offer gifts to certain people? Would he change the rate of taxation? Would he declare war on an enemy?

Well, at the time there were few who could see the significance of his first key action. But I knew what he would do before it was even announced. One major city remained in Gentile hands. It was there – right in the centre of the Promised Land – as a testimony to the failure of Israel to fulfil the commands of God, and a demonstration that the flesh is, at times, mighty and powerful. It was a living, breathing manifestation of sin in our country. Evil men taunted us from that place, stating how powerful they were and how we would never be able to defeat them. Which city was this? Jebus – named after the Jebusites who had possessed it for hundreds of years. The time had come for this city to be taken by God's chosen people at last.

The decision to liberate Jebus was not taken lightly by David. It was an awesome citadel, built on a series of hills, and it was said to be impregnable. Others – judges, rulers and kings – had attempted to capture this place. Every one of them had failed. If David's rule over all Israel began with a botched attempt to conquer this city, what would people say or think? How would they react to him as their king? If he didn't succeed, would some reject him as their ruler altogether? We needn't have worried. David had been commanded to take the city by the Lord. And no walls and towers – however strong or high – were going to stand in the way of our God and His chosen ruler.

David called his mighty men to stand before him. We were all very well aware of the importance of this, and waited for him to reveal what he had planned.

"My mighty men, my friends, my brothers. These are momentous days for us all. By God's grace I am now the king over all Israel and am determined to rule in righteousness and fairness. And in this, I will need your help and support. You will be acting as my ambassadors in the nation, as you have done already in Judah. Together, and particularly with God's blessing, we can make this nation greater, more powerful and, most importantly, more faithful."

There were cries of agreement. We all knew what an important time this was: for Israel, for David, and for every one of us. Our lord continued,

"As a young man, I sometimes took my sheep to the area around the city of Jebus. I vowed that if ever I had the opportunity to do so, I would seek to purify that place – to cast out Gentile rule. Now the time has come for that vow to be fulfilled. We march for Jebus in the morning."

The journey up from Hebron was uneventful. But, as soon as we saw the city, with its massive walls and great iron gates, we wondered why we had bothered travelling so far! How would anyone be able to scale those walls? We looked up and saw certain Jebusites taunting us. One cried that he had placed a blind watchman on duty, and another stated that the guards were all lame. This is how confident they felt. This was the challenge we faced.

That night, David called us together once more. Without that city being under Israelite rule, we couldn't even be certain that he would be accepted by many of the people of Israel – the Benjamites, especially.

"The one who gains access to Jebus will be my army commander", declared the king. "I vow before Almighty God – the man who enters the city will lead my army."

We all gazed up at Jebus again. Surely this was impossible? How could any man accomplish that ascent without being seen? David continued his challenge,

"Men, there is only one way in. Someone must climb up that water shaft – the conduit which connects the city with the outside world."

Again, I couldn't see how anyone would ever manage such a feat. That shaft – like a large drain pipe – was hardly any wider than a man's body. Scaling it would be impossible, surely? Well, one man amongst our number clearly had the ability and courage to make that daring assault. And while we all waited down below, he managed to climb up that pipe, gain access to the city, and open the gates to the rest of us who were waiting down below.

I saw the look on David's face. He was overjoyed that the city could now be taken but, I suspected, grieved that Joab – of all men – was the one who had managed to enter it and open the gates. But David had vowed a vow, and he had to fulfil it. Joab would command his armies.

"Never break your word, Hez", he said to me on more than one occasion. "A man who doesn't keep his word is nothing. Nothing at all. Our gracious Father is a God who is abundant in goodness and truth. If we wish to please Him, this is the standard we need to aim for. Without truth, goodness is an impossibility."

A few hours after this incident, the king spoke with Joab at great length about what he expected of him as his army commander. David was very explicit about what would and wouldn't be acceptable. Whether these words achieved anything, I can't say. I know that my heart sank when I saw Joab up there, waving for us to come up and defeat the enemy. Anyone – anyone but Joab. But it had to be.

It didn't take long for us to swarm in through those great gates and destroy those who had taunted us from the position of strength. Psalms rang out from the City of God that night! After so many years, Jebus was ours! Now, at last, it could become that place of peace.

As soon as the Philistines heard that David had been made king over the whole land, they gathered, ready for war. This was no idle show on their part. The whole army was called – every single fighting man. They were clearly determined to show that they would not accept this new ruler's authority. The place where they assembled could hardly have been more significant – Rephaim, the Valley of the Giants. Maybe they wanted to show that, although David had killed one giant, there were plenty more still to come!

Our lord, wisely, asked for guidance from God. He was told to attack the enemy at a specific location in the valley. As expected, David gathered the army together. He encouraged us, assuring us that we were not simply fighting to secure our borders – we were fighting for the lives of our families. But, more than this, we were going into battle bearing the name of Yahweh, Israel's God. We went as His warriors – His representatives. We were not simply David's mighty men. We were the mighty ones of Israel's God.

Not long after the battle started, I knew we would win. What followed was an overwhelming, crushing victory for Israel. We lost only a few men. Many thousands of Philistines lay dead. The key location of our victory became known as Baalperazim – or "lord of the breaches". There had been a 'breach' in the enemy lines, and David had seized the opportunity to force his way through. All the Philistines' pagan idols were lined up, five great fish-gods, called Dagon – one from each major city. We managed to reach them, knocked them to the ground, broke them to pieces and burned them. After that, it was easy.

Well, the Philistines refused to give up. They regrouped, repaired their chariots and weapons, and gathered once more – again a massive number of men spread out in the Valley of the Giants. And again David asked for guidance from God before going into battle.

This time, the instructions from the Father were, it has to be said, a little unusual. We were told to march to the rear of the valley so that the Philistines were encamped in front of us. And we were to wait. We weren't allowed to go forward, fire an arrow, or make any sound, until we heard the noise of an army marching. We were told that this sound would be heard in the tops of the trees which grew around the valley. Some of the younger, less experienced men were a bit unsure. Some had to be physically restrained. We knew that if the Philistines were to turn round and see us, we would be trapped – enemy soldiers in front and the enemy land behind us. Yet we had been told to wait in silence and in faith. And so this is what we did.

It was as the sun began to rise on the second day that we heard the sound. It began quietly, but then grew to a tumultuous explosion of noise. A gigantic army was marching, right above us. The angels of God had gone forth, and we were to follow! With a great roar we leapt from our places and ran towards the Philistine soldiers. The noise alone had left them petrified. When they saw us racing towards them, with David and Joab at the head, it was too much! They tried to flee, but that meant they were heading towards Israel, where more of our men were stationed.

The battle which followed was a further glorious triumph for Israel as a whole, and for David particularly. It set the scene for much of what was to come afterwards. Gentile nations were, for the most part, terrified of doing anything which might offend him in any way. What a start to his reign over all the twelve tribes!

What came next was even more wonderful. The city of Jebus – now renamed Jerusalem, Zion or even at times, "the City of David", was rebuilt and purified. Under the Jebusites parts of it had been untouched for many years. The walls of a number of the buildings were broken down. Gates and doors were rotten. Open sewers caused the whole city to stink. For the next few years we worked tirelessly, cleansing this place, making it fit for a king – our king. Joab who, to his credit, seemed to have taken to heart at least some of the things that David had said to him, was an extremely skilled stonemason. Under him, great sections of the walls were rebuilt.

"It's as though the stones are coming back to life, Hez", remarked Ahithophel, as he surveyed our work.

"This is the place from which the Messiah will reign, one day. Zion will be his capital city. That's when the whole world will know of our God and His plan and purpose. Eventually, the entire planet will glorify Him. But it will all start at Zion. This is the key location. This is the City of the Great King."

The ark of the covenant – the holiest item in all Israel – was still in a tent at Gibeah. Nothing necessarily wrong with that. After all, it had been in a tent, or tabernacle, since it had been made, when the nation was in the wilderness. The ark was a wooden chest, covered with gold, with various important items inside and two solid gold 'Cherubim' on top. They were representations of the power of God – and all who tried to be like Him – the promised Messiah, especially.

I used to sit with Ahithophel and other elders – a great man called Hushai particularly – and listen to them explaining why the Cherubim were so important. At first, I struggled to get it. 'Creatures' with four different faces: a lion, an eagle, an ox and a man. What could this possibly mean? Finally, I managed to see that this showed Israel what the Messiah would be like. Although he would be a man, he would be as far-sighted as an eagle, as courageous as a lion, and with the strength of an ox. Ultimately, Hushai explained, this described the Messiah in his immortal state.

From the day the city was taken, it had always been David's intention to bring the ark up to Jerusalem. He tried to do so once, but that came to nothing. In hindsight, the method of transportation had been wrong. I know my lord accepted this afterwards. It had been placed on a cart which was pulled by two oxen. When the oxen stumbled, a man called Uzzah reached out to steady the ark, thinking it was about to fall. He was immediately killed by God.

David was afraid to move the ark after this. It was left in the house of a great man called Obed-edom. He was a Gittite. For the next few months the whole family of this man was blessed – and this prompted David to determine once more to relocate the ark to its rightful resting place within the holy city.

That triumphal entry of the ark of the covenant was one of the most dramatic, exciting and uplifting things I have ever experienced. Many, many thousands of men and women were gathered together, singing and

The ark was a wooden chest, covered with gold, with various important items inside and two solid gold 'Cherubim' on top

praising the Lord. All around trumpets sounded out. David led the procession, stopping to rejoice before the Almighty at regular intervals – singing psalms of glory, offering sacrifices or giving gifts to the people. He had been instructed by God to wear a linen ephod, which was the garment of a priest. Some may have questioned this. After all, he was a king, not a priest. But we could all see why this was so right. Bringing that ark – the holiest item in Israel – into the greatest city in the world was a pointer forward to an even greater time.

"It has to be, Hez", said Hushai, as we paused, taking in the sights and sounds on our approach to Zion that amazing day.

"The Messiah will be a king and a priest, and he will possess this very city one day. Abraham's seed will come and reign, sitting in the gate of his enemies. This is a small representation of what that awesome time will be like. All the faithful ones will be with him then. All will glorify him and the one true God. What a time that will be."

As I listened to the singing and looked around at the people gathered together, I found it hard to get my head round this. These events were so wonderful, so glorious, so breathtaking – in every way right and holy – and yet something far, far better would come one day!

Chapter 15

Promises of glory

THE NEXT few years were mostly a time of peace, prosperity and joy in God's land. David's administration moved from Hebron to Jerusalem, and the nation continued to develop in many ways. Our borders were secured, and the people were, generally speaking, happy, faithful and prosperous.

The practice of having a number of mighty men stationed with the king and his family was maintained. It had worked so well during our time in Hebron, and David was determined that this should continue. So for three months of the year I was with him at the palace. For the other nine months I lived at Carmel. Nabal's land had been left barren since Abigail had married my lord. Once the kingdom was established, she said that she wanted the land to be managed properly again ... and that she wanted to give it to me. I was speechless. All those years before I had worked in those fields for a few coins a week – and now the whole area was to be mine! Initially, I wasn't sure, and I expressed my doubts to Abigail.

"But Hez, I really want you to have it", she explained. "I could sell it if I wanted to, but how could I be sure that the new owners would be fair and merciful? The people of Carmel need someone who will look after their best interests – someone who will show the kindness of God in his dealings with them. I know I can trust you to do this for me."

In many ways this was typical of this marvellous, beautiful, godly woman. Yes, she could have made a reasonable amount of money by selling the whole site – but it was far more important to her that the land was farmed ethically, and that the people who depended on it for their livelihoods were helped, encouraged and loved. Once I had composed myself I thanked her for her incredible generosity, and assured her that I would do everything in my power to live up to her high standards.

I remembered how she had cared for those in need, and I smiled. I particularly recalled the time she had taken pity on a poor, scruffy, uncouth orphan boy who had wanted to buy a tent but couldn't afford to do so (and then was too blind to see that he had been the recipient of a wonderfully generous act!). I vowed before the God of Abraham that I would do everything in my power to be like her in my management of the land and my treatment of others.

As soon as I arrived back in Carmel, I visited Aunty Jemima. Uncle Jed had died the year before. It didn't come as a surprise to me or anyone else who knew him. It's just not possible for a man to poison his system with that much alcohol – day after day, year after year – and not pay the price. I was away on the king's business in Lebanon and didn't hear about his death until I had returned, so I wasn't able to be present at the funeral. I understand that it was a sombre occasion.

As I sat in the family home in Carmel, virtually unchanged since the time I had lived there, I remember thinking that Aunty Jem looked as though a gigantic weight had been lifted from her shoulders. She was certainly a very different person from the one I had known all those years before.

When I lived with her, she had very literally, tiptoed around, afraid that her husband would rise from his slumber and begin to berate her or me. I'd never actually seen him do so, but I strongly suspected that he hit her at times. She had lived her entire married life in a state of abject poverty. But now she was free. And, thanks to the generosity of some in the city who had very kindly sent gifts of food, clothing or money to her following the funeral, she was in a position to start again. I did my best to help her as much as I could, with repairs to the house and items of food. I offered to move back in with her, but she wouldn't even consider it.

"Oh, Hez, you have your own life to live", she told me. "You don't want to waste your time looking after an old widow like me. I'll be fine."

In fact, within just a few weeks of Uncle Jed's death, things started to look up for her. Her twin sister, Deborah, (who she loved dearly, but Uncle Jed hated the sight of) had moved in with her and they were a source of great strength and encouragement to each other. She had let out the vineyard to the family who lived next door, cultivated a section of the garden for herbs, and had bought herself a loom. Before she had married she had worked as a weaver. She had even brought an old loom with her when she had moved to Carmel, but that had been sold by Uncle Jed within a month of the marriage taking place. You can probably guess what he spent the money on.

I called to see her as often as possible, and noted the improvement in her circumstances over the following weeks and months. The house and surrounding area were tidy with everything in its place. The herb garden was thriving. The loom was always busy. Such was the quality of the items she produced, she usually had a steady stream of customers. The vineyard was totally transformed. Great, beautiful, healthy vines grew steadily. The tower and winepress were repaired. A solid stone wall had been built right around the site. I could hardly believe it was the same place.

"What did I say to you all those years ago?" she asked me one day. "I told you that you would achieve greatness. And I was right. Just look at you now – a mighty man in the administration of the king, and a landowner with fields, servants and animals."

"You also encouraged me to believe in the Almighty", I said, hugging her, "to pray to Him and to seek to serve Him. It took me a long time to get there, but I managed it at last."

The land which had been the property of Nabal and Abigail was in a terrible state when I arrived. Walls and fences were down. Gates and grain-stores burned to the ground. Sheepfolds crumbling. Fields left fallow for year after year, and animals running wild. It took three whole years to turn things around. Some of the locals said I would never manage it. But, with God's blessing, and with an enormous amount of hard work and help, I did.

Shortly after the ark had arrived in Jerusalem I was on my way back to Carmel and stopped off in Hebron to catch up with the Boss and Han. As always, they were delighted to see me. Their granddaughter, Naamah, was staying with them for a few weeks. She and her parents lived in the neighbouring village of Mareshah, but she was helping Han at the inn. Straight away I knew she was someone I wanted to get to know. It wasn't just that she was pretty; she was also kind. I saw that in her dealings with her younger brothers and sisters – but also with the Boss and Han.

Over the next few months I never missed a chance to visit Carmel or, if Naamah was back home, Mareshah. There had been lots of single young women in the Kahal, and I got on very well with many of them. I knew, from what others had said to me, that some of them really liked me. But I wasn't interested. Partly because of the hardness of our way of life. More because they didn't seem to be right for me. But somehow, Naamah was different. She wanted to talk with me about the Law and the promises to Abraham. We chatted about David and the city of Jerusalem. We spoke for hours about life in the Kahal and what it was like being chased by Saul. Within three months we were betrothed. Inside a year we were married. David kindly attended our wedding in

Mareshah. I know he had plenty of other things which demanded his attention, but he said he wouldn't have missed it for anything. It was a fantastic day.

Having lived as a single man for so long, it took me a while to get used to certain aspects of married life. I'd been so very selfish for most of my life – doing things my own way, without a care for others or their feelings. Now I had to learn to put Naamah first. But the privileges of married life far outweighed any 'disadvantages'! The love we shared was wonderful, precious, pure. Oh, how I had been blessed! I got down on my knees and thanked God every single day for what I had.

Around this time, all the mighty men were called to stand before the king in Jerusalem. We knew straight away that this had to be important. Since the repairs to the city of Zion had been completed, we hadn't been together in one place at the same time.

We were invited to meet in the great hall – and, seeing all of the Gibbor in one location, it took me right back! How things had changed since those days when we had lived in the forests, desperate to stay one step ahead of Saul and his men. We had suffered all sorts of extremes of weather, and lack of food. Sometimes I was so tired I didn't think I could put one foot in front of another. And yet, hard though those times were, they had done so much to shape us as individuals and to bind us together as a unit. I genuinely believed that every single man in that room would do anything for our lord and for the other members of the Gibbor. That's how strong the bond of love and fellowship was between us.

*The love we shared was wonderful,
precious, pure*

"Hez, it's good to see you."

I turned and saw Joab, with Abishai.

"Joab, Abishai, you look well", I said – and they did. In many ways Joab resembled David physically. Both were tall and had fine, broad shoulders. Both had clear, olive skin, with strong features. Both had dark hair and beards, with only a bit of grey. They were, without question, fine-looking men.

"This city is amazing", I continued. "I can hardly believe what you've been able to achieve – especially when I think what it was like when we first gained access to it."

Joab smiled. He really seemed to have changed. I was pleased. We chatted about things to do with the kingdom for a few minutes. Then one of the other men called Abishai over and I was left alone with Joab.

"Now that it's just you and me, there's something I've been meaning to say to you for some time", he said, sounding rather hesitant. I was a little surprised. What could he possibly have to say to me?

"Many years ago, you reprimanded me for speaking inappropriately about our lord. Now – and I really mean this – thank you. Very few of the others have the guts to stand up to me. You did. You were right, and I was wrong. I admire your spirit, Hez. Never let anyone quench it. You're a true mighty man. And you never know when we may be called upon to fight for our lord again."

He reached out and placed a hand on my shoulder.

"Great to see you again", he said, and smiled. "Oh – and congratulations on your marriage, by the way. I hope you'll both be very happy."

With that he turned away, and I was left, stunned. Did he truly mean what he had just said? Well, I had to believe so! And coming from a man like Joab, this was an astonishing – yet extremely encouraging – thing to hear.

I had heard that others from our group had also married recently. Uriah, for example, had wed a stunningly beautiful young woman called Bathsheba. She was the granddaughter of Ahithophel and 'the apple of his eye'. I had been told that, if Granddad hadn't approved of her choice of husband, the marriage would never have taken place! I could see Uriah at the other side of the room and was about to make my way over when an announcement was made; we were to take our seats, as the king had something that he needed to tell us.

David appeared on a wooden stage raised about five feet above the level of the main hall. Also with him were the prophet Nathan, the wise man Ahithophel, and Abiathar the priest. This was clearly a very important issue. The whole room went silent. David stood up,

"My friends ... my brothers. You have been with me through so much. We have experienced times of ease and joy, and times of hardship and sorrow. A man may live his entire life without meeting anyone he really trusts – anyone who would be willing to sacrifice his life for him. And in this room, there are a great number of mighty ones – men with whom I have, and would, trust my very life."

Many in the audience indicated our approval. We all knew these things were true, but it was an honour to hear it – especially from someone as great as David.

"Now, certain things have been revealed to me by God through the prophet Nathan, and as you have been with me for so very long, I thought it only right that I make you all aware of them at the same time. Hardly anyone else in the kingdom knows this ... yet. You can, if you wish, pass this information on to others in the towns and villages of Israel in the coming weeks and months. And now I would like to invite the prophet Nathan to speak to you."

We all remained totally silent while the prophet addressed us.

"Mighty men of our lord, thank you for your company today. Some weeks ago, our king made me aware of his desire to build a great temple for Yahweh, our God, here in Zion. For reasons which I won't go into now, he wasn't permitted to do this. But our Heavenly Father has made certain promises to him, and we feel that you should be aware of these great things."

We sat and listened, stunned at what had been promised to David. We always knew that he was special – a man unlike any other. But he had been told by God, through Nathan, that one of his descendants would be the Messiah. This one, unique, promised child would reign on David's throne (or, more correctly, his re-created throne) in Zion for ever. Israel would finally be at peace. But more than that – the promised seed would also be the son of God – a descendant of David through his mother. But the father of this one, special son would be the Almighty Himself. We were so taken aback by these amazing things that we had to ask Nathan to repeat them, in case we had misheard. But we hadn't. They really were true.

Ahithophel stood up next. He gave further details about this one promised seed – where he would be born, and how this would come about. He told us openly that, although some of the things which had been revealed would have an application to David's immediate family, in their fullest sense they spoke only of one who would come many years later.

It was Abiathar's turn next. He explained that this "son of God and son of David" would be the one through whom salvation and redemption would be possible – not only for Israel, but also for all mankind.

As I sat there, amazed by these awesome things, I wondered how the Gibbor would react. At first, we just sat there in silence. Then one man stood up. It was Benaiah. He requested permission to approach the front and address the group. We all waited while he made his way to the front of the room.

"My brothers and my friends", he said. "What a privilege this is! Not only that our lord should be selected to be the beneficiary of these amazing things – but that he should choose to reveal them to us first. Truly we are of all men greatly blessed!"

We all stood up and cheered. After this, Benaiah gave a short, extremely moving prayer, reflecting the thoughts of many in the room. We then praised our Heavenly Father, singing a number of the psalms of David, rejoicing at the goodness of God and how His love had been poured out on us sinful, mortal men.

We stayed at Jerusalem for just one night and then returned to our home cities with a spring in our steps and a song in our hearts. David's house would continue forever, the Messiah would be born of his line – and the Gibbor had been chosen as some of the first people to know these wonderful things!

Chapter 16

One man's weakness, and the consequences for others

THE GREAT man Ahithophel was speaking about sin. A number of the people had gathered together, there in the synagogue at Carmel. To be honest, I had hoped that more would attend, but it's not possible to force any man or woman to learn or to serve. It has to be their choice. Some of these things I had heard before. Others were totally new to me. They were fascinating – but also slightly worrying!

"Sin takes many forms", Ahithophel explained. "And it can strike at any time. Sometimes when we feel we are at our strongest – that's when it traps us. But there are sins that some of us find easier to resist than others. One man may be tempted to drink heavily. He may struggle with this for his entire life, sometimes succumbing. Others are not tempted in the slightest to drink to excess. It doesn't affect them in the same way."

I thought back to my childhood in Carmel and Uncle Jed. I had always condemned him as a pathetic waste of space – only interested in wine and nothing else. But maybe he really struggled with this? Maybe he knew it was wrong and had tried very hard to resist?

"Very simply, temptation can be divided into three different groups", explained Ahithophel. "And I believe that we are all likely to fail in one of these areas. Some are tempted by great wealth. They want to be rich – or, more probably, they want to be richer than everyone else. Others are proud. They take offence very easily. They find it hard to forgive or forget. They cherish a desire to get even if they feel they have been wronged. Others are tempted by the things of the flesh – by a desire to satisfy physical desires. A man may be very happily married, yet he might still look on another woman and long to be with her. And that longing may result in taking and acting."

One of the men in the audience was Joab. David had insisted that one of the Gibbor had to travel with Ahithophel wherever he went. Many said he was like an angel of God, and our lord would not risk him being killed or captured by enemies of the Crown. His words were so powerful – yet so relevant. And he could get down to anyone's level. I once heard him talking to a group of five and six-year-olds about the flood. They sat transfixed; all of them hanging on his every word.

He then went on to connect this teaching about sin to events in the Garden of Eden. He explained how important it is that we are aware of our weaknesses – not necessarily the weaknesses of others. He said how easy it is for us to spot flaws in those around us, while being unable to see our own failings. He stressed that our God is a God of mercy and love, who forgives where there is a genuine confession of sin and repentance ... but He takes no pleasure in the actions of those who continue to do wrong, all the time claiming that they are right. Such people will be judged for their hard-heartedness.

At the end of the talk, Ahithophel made his way to our house, where he was staying for a few days. He had other talks to give locally, and this was his base during this time. A little like Samuel when I was a boy, this great man travelled from place to place, teaching, encouraging and offering words of guidance in cases where a judgment had to be made. His words about sin and temptation remained with me. I knew very well where I had failed. As a proud man (at times I had even been called arrogant) I was very reluctant to forgive others if I felt I had been treated badly. Even when I knew I was in the wrong, I would often refuse to apologise or back down. I knew how wrong this was and from that day on I determined to try to be more repentant – and humble.

Apart from the three months a year when I was at Zion, I spent most of my time in Carmel. But as a mighty man – one of David's own private guard – I had to be ready to fight at any time. There had been wars against a number of surrounding nations in the early years of David's reign. The Philistines, Moabites, Syrians, Edomites and others had all been defeated.

On one occasion David had sent a message of comfort to a new king in Ammon, following his father's death. This had been misunderstood entirely by the Ammonites, and the men from Israel who had been sent from David were treated very badly. What followed was an enormous battle between the two nations. The Ammonites hired a large number of mercenaries to fight alongside them. The call had already gone out for all the mighty men to report to the palace. We were divided into two groups: one under Joab's command and one led by his brother Abishai.

The resulting battle raged for many days. I'd rarely seen so many enemy soldiers in one place – a massive numbers of horses and chariots. They were clearly very capable and experienced – and determined to shed Israelite blood. It was then that the character of Joab – his awesome ability as an army commander – came to the fore. Before the conflict began he gave such a rousing speech that even the most feeble of men would have felt able to face the coming days with confidence. He ensured that the Gibbor were dispersed evenly throughout the army, and told those who were less experienced to follow our example. He was to lead the assault against the Syrians. Abishai would attack the Ammonites. They agreed that if either was struggling, they would signal for support from the other.

"Be strong, Israelites", he cried. "Follow the mighty men. Be like them. Fight for your families, your cities, your king and your God. And may Yahweh our God reward you."

Although the battle that followed was long and bloody, it was also a resounding victory for Israel. We lost some men. Others were so badly wounded that

The resulting battle raged for many days

they were unable to fight again. But generally speaking, these incidents were rare. Thousands of Ammonites and Syrians were killed. Towards the end of the first full week, Joab sent a message to David, asking him to rally the rest of the nation – to gather all the other fighting men – and come down to support us. In the conflict that followed, forty thousand warriors from Syria were killed, including their army commander. Never again did the Syrians come against Israel in our lifetime. What a victory! What a day!

The Syrians were dealt with, but that still left the Ammonites. Their royal city was Rabbah – a massive place, with great strong walls, gigantic iron gates and fortified towers. We knew that, unless we managed to gain access to it, they would only regroup, hire more mercenaries from other lands and attack us again. Many of the men of Israel had returned home with David. That left the mighty men and another few thousand foot soldiers, encamped around the city walls. I imagined that, if we received word that battle was about to commence, we would call for reinforcements.

For the next few days we remained in our places. A few arrows were fired into and out of the city, but nothing more. Reports were sent back to Jerusalem every day. Unusually, Uriah was called to return to Zion on one occasion. I assumed this was so that he could relay details of the conflict to the king. He remained there for three days, and then joined us again on the battlefield. I suspected that it would only be a matter of days before the city's defences were breached, and then we would be in.

But things didn't proceed as I had expected. Instead of the Ammonites coming out as one, or remaining in the city and trying to wait out the siege, they would send out bands of thirty or forty men to attack us.

On one occasion I was with about another ten men, fighting with a slightly larger number of very capable, well-equipped Ammonite warriors. Joab and Uriah were in our group. We found ourselves backed into a corner, just outside the city walls. As well as contending with enemy soldiers in front of us, arrows and boulders rained down from above. The resulting conflict was extremely intense and bloody. Men fell on both sides. When it became apparent that we needed to regroup, Joab called for us to retreat. But to my horror, I looked back and saw that we had left one man behind! Uriah was alone. He was a short distance away from us and surrounded by Ammonites. More than that, he was badly injured. Two arrows were embedded in his right arm and another in one of his legs.

"My lord Joab, this isn't right", I cried. "We never leave a man alone. We are the mighty men. We can't do this!"

"Hez, we have our instructions", he replied. "We must retreat. I don't like it any more than you do. But we must back off."

At that point he and another man quite literally dragged me out of the battle. One of my legs was wounded and I was struggling to walk anyway, but I didn't care. What mattered to me was Uriah. And I knew that without back-up he wouldn't have a chance. No man, however faithful, courageous or capable, can withstand that many foes if he is seriously injured. Uriah, this wonderfully brave warrior – this giant of faith who had rejected the gods of the Hittites and embraced Israel's Hope – was dead.

As soon as we were back in the camp, I requested a meeting with Joab. He was the army commander and I had to respect that. But what had happened was wrong – all wrong.

"My lord", I said, determined not to lose my cool, "what happened back there? Why did you leave a faithful man to die? Uriah is one of the Gibbor, and you know our creed – we never turn our backs on one of our own."

For a few seconds he was silent. He stood with his back to me. Then, very slowly, he turned around.

"Hez, I'm only going to say this to you once", he replied. He spoke quietly, slowly, and with great feeling. I was amazed to see that there were tears in his eyes. Never had I seen him moved like this before.

"The command came to me from above. I feel just as bad as you do about this. It was the last thing in the world I wanted to do. But I had no choice. Remember what Ahithophel said, that day in Carmel, about different kinds of temptation? Now – I'm asking you, please, never speak to me about this again."

With that, he turned away. I could see his great shoulders shaking. He didn't make a sound, but there was no question about it; he was sobbing like a child.

I wandered back to my tent in a daze. What on earth had happened over the last few hours? What could Joab possibly have meant – "an instruction from above"? Who was above him but the king? But why would David want any Israelite dead? Especially one of his mightiest, most faithful followers? Why would he arrange the death of a man who had been with him through so much? A man who had put his life on the line for him time and again? It didn't make any sense.

I lay awake all that night, going over and over the events of that awful day. And still I couldn't work it out. Maybe Joab was lying? And yet he had given every impression that he was telling the truth. Or maybe (and this really was too terrible to contemplate) David really did want Uriah dead. But why?

A few weeks after this Joab sent a message to David to say that he had to come and oversee the final assault on Rabbah. The people inside were getting desperate, and it seemed only a matter of time before the walls were breached and we would be in. A couple of days later, David arrived with the rest of the army and the city was taken. The King of Ammon was cornered, and David removed the royal crown from his head. It was an act of great significance. That man had no power before Israel's mighty king.

So within a matter of days, we had returned to Israel, victorious. Those around me sang for joy as we crossed the Jordan and made our way back to Jerusalem, and then to our own cities. But I couldn't join in those times of celebration.

The more I thought about it, the more worried I became. I couldn't avoid the shocking conclusion that David had been behind the death of Uriah – that he had expressly told Joab how to act so that a faithful man would lose his life. But why? It couldn't be because Uriah had offended him in any way. David wasn't like that. And even if he had broken one of the key commandments under the Law, Uriah would have been tried and then stoned to death. Did David want Uriah dead because of something that the mighty man knew about him? And if so, what could that possibly be? Again, I just couldn't think of any set of circumstances which would fit in with this.

I had been back in Carmel for a couple of days when another possibility came to me. I remembered how Joab had mentioned Ahithophel's talk about sin, when he was in Carmel. I recalled what the great man had said – that some men may be weak in relation to the things of the flesh. A man may covet another man's wife, and take steps to have her.

It was, surely, unthinkable. Terrible. Horrifying! And yet, as I gazed upon Naamah, admiring the beauty of her features, it suddenly fell into place. If another man coveted her and was determined to have her, then he would have to remove me in order for his desires to be satisfied. Had David coveted Bathsheba and killed Uriah so that he could have her for his wife? It seemed too ridiculous to be true. This was the one who had been called "a man after God's own heart". And he had received all those awesome promises, speaking of him and his family for many years to come.

Yet within a few weeks, the news came to me that I had been dreading. Bathsheba, Uriah's widow, had married David and was expecting a child. I never said a word to anyone about my suspicions, not even Naamah. But I knew in my heart that something very wrong had taken place. And if David had committed adultery with another man's wife and then had him killed so that he might have her as his own, I knew that the Law of Moses demanded death.

I didn't know what to do or say. What I did know was that, if the king had acted so inappropriately, there would be consequences. Little did I or anyone else know just how life-changing those consequences would be – for David, and for those closest to him.

Chapter 17

David's confession

ON MY first visit to the capital after the death of Uriah, I was summoned to stand before the king. I wasn't really surprised by this; something had to be said. Following their marriage, Bathsheba's son had, sadly, died when he was just seven days old. To those who knew no better, David had merely married a beautiful widow, and she had lost her first child. I knew it wasn't that simple. If I was right about the king ... then how could he possibly continue to rule the nation? What about the Law? We all knew what it said: those guilty of adultery – male and female – had to die. And those who murder must also be stoned. It was black and white.

That initial meeting with the king was, unsurprisingly, more than a little uncomfortable. There were twelve of us there – David, Nathan, and ten of the Gibbor. We were invited to sit with the king, who said that he had something he needed to explain to us. I'd never seen him like this. For a while he wasn't able to look any of us in the eye. He struggled to find the right words.

"My mighty men ... I thank God, as always, for your love and support. Now, I need to make you aware of certain events which have taken place, and how they have impacted upon me and those closest to me. If, when you have heard what I have to say, you wish to resign your positions and return home, I will understand entirely. I give you my word that I won't hold it against you."

I was fairly certain that I already knew what he was about to say. Whether the others had also worked it out, I wasn't sure.

"The flesh we bear is a vile and evil thing", he told us. "You have heard it said that serving God is like fighting a battle. Well, some months ago, I have to confess to you that I stopped fighting that battle altogether. I gave in to a weak, sinful desire and committed an act which had very, very serious repercussions – for me and for others as well."

There were tears in his eyes. It was then that he looked up and gazed directly at me.

"I looked upon the wife of another man and instead of looking away, I took her and committed adultery with her. Shortly after this she sent a message to me, explaining that she was pregnant. The child was mine. There was no question about it. Her husband hadn't been at home for almost a year. I am so ashamed of how I behaved at that time. In desperation, I arranged for her husband to be killed. I then married her, and she gave birth to a son. Very sadly, he died when he was only seven days old."

He began to weep. We all sat there, waiting for him to continue. Finally, he composed himself.

"That man ... that man was Uriah the Hittite. The woman was Bathsheba. My friends, I can find no words to excuse my actions. These things will live with me forever. At first I refused even to accept that I had done wrong but thankfully, the prophet Nathan was sent by Almighty God with a message for me, and I confessed my sin. I would do anything to change what happened. Uriah was one of the greatest men I've ever met. I truly believe that when the Messiah comes, he will be raised from the dead and granted immortality. But he now sleeps in the earth. His death was down to me, and nobody else. No matter how or where he died, I was entirely responsible."

After a few seconds' silence, David took his seat, and Nathan stood up.

"Men of the Gibbor. I know we can trust you to be wise and discreet regarding this matter. Our king was made aware of his sin and immediately acknowledged that he had done wrong. A message came to me straight away: that Yahweh, our merciful Heavenly Father, had put away his sin. He did not need to die for his actions. This is, I believe, an example of a greater law than the one we seek to keep now – a new law altogether, where grace and love are at the forefront of things. Now that you have been made aware of the facts, you need to decide how to behave. I would ask you to return to your rooms and pray about what you have heard, then meet back here tomorrow morning as soon as you hear the sound of the cockerels crowing."

With that, he offered a short prayer and we all dispersed throughout the city. I lay in bed that night, staring at the ceiling. What I had just heard was terrible – but in truth, I knew it already. What had been revealed had simply confirmed what I had suspected for the last few months. I prayed and prayed, asking that I might have the strength to do what was right.

The next day we gathered in the same hall. David sat before us once again. He seemed to have aged over these last few months. Bearing in mind that meetings like this one may already have taken place with other groups (and there would probably be more still to be arranged), I suppose this was understandable.

"My mighty men", he said. "I have confessed my sin before our God, and I have made you aware of it as well. I am not in a position to command you to do anything concerning this matter. But I need to know if I can still count on your loyalty."

Immediately I rose from my place. I tried hard to fight back the tears, but they just kept coming.

"My lord and my king", I said, "as you know, Uriah and I were extremely close. I never had a brother, but he was a brother to me – and so much more. He was a brave, faithful, kind and generous man. But you are my lord, the anointed of God, and I know you have repented of your actions. If our Heavenly Father has forgiven you, then how can I hold a grudge? Our God is a God of mercy and love. We all need His goodness. We all need to try to forgive others if they have wronged us. And I thank you for trusting us sufficiently to tell us the truth. I appreciate how hard this meeting has been for you."

One by one the others stood up. They all indicated their agreement with what I had said.

David fell to his knees and sobbed. I didn't want this. It wasn't my intention to make him feel small or sinful. But I could see how much this meant to him. I was grateful that at least I knew exactly what had happened and that my lord was genuinely repentant. At last I felt I could move on. David rose up and, one by one he hugged us, thanking us for our support and love.

I could only imagine how Bathsheba must have felt. She had lost a wonderful husband and also her firstborn son. Most, if not all in the palace must have known what had happened while her husband was away from home. In fairness to David, he treated her the same as his other wives – maybe even better than some of them. She was never shunned or neglected because of what had gone on between them. Within a few years they were blessed with a number of sons. One of them, Solomon, was an amazing young man – kind, faithful, and with an astonishing thirst for knowledge. He would sit for hours with Hushai, talking about the history of the nation, and the law.

Over the coming years, life in the kingdom continued, following a precisely defined pattern. Cities were built or repaired. Borders were made secure. Areas of land which had become barren deserts were irrigated and came back to life again. The army was strengthened, with stores of weapons being stockpiled and men trained. We had to be ready for anything. The mighty men were always involved in this process. We would recruit and train new soldiers, always stressing the importance of trusting in the Almighty and fighting for Him. When an Israelite went to war, we told them he did so in the name of Israel's God. There were no major conflicts during these years. A few minor skirmishes – disputes over border towns – but nothing much apart from that. These were, thankfully, days of peace and prosperity in God's land.

I still spent three months at Jerusalem and the rest of the year with my family in Carmel. By this time Naamah and I had been blessed with three fantastic daughters. We named the oldest Hanniah, after the Boss's wife and Naamah's grandmother, who had done so much to make me feel welcome in Hebron. After her came the twins: Leah and Elisheba. Our son, who was given the family name Hezrai had, very sadly, died three days after his birth. For many months a sense of gloom descended over the entire house in Carmel. But Naamah was so faithful throughout this time. She was the one who encouraged me that we had to believe in God's goodness and grace, and that we needed to ensure that the girls were encouraged and loved. Slowly, taking it one day at a time, we managed to get back to some sort of normality. We hoped and prayed for another son to continue the family name.

By now David's family was enormous! As king of the land he had many wives and concubines and, of course, lots of children. They were granted special blessings by their father, but he always ensured that they knew the importance of faithful service. Yes, they were children of the king, but that didn't give them the right to abuse their positions of power. His sons were all sent to spend time with the army. We were told to treat them like any other new recruit. They had to know how to fight. They needed to be ready to wage war in the service of the Lord, if this was required.

Most of these young men were hardly any different from the others who came to us. Some had a bit of an attitude. They clearly believed that they should be able to do things their own way. It didn't take them long to see that we weren't going to be bossed about by anyone – not even by the sons of the king of all Israel! After the first few weeks, most of them were fine. There was only one who was different. His name was Absalom. Right from the start, I suspected that he was going to be trouble.

As he grew, it became very clear to all who met him that Absalom was an astonishing young man. He was of royal descent on both sides: his mother was the daughter of the king of an area called Geshur, which was to the north-east of Israel. He was supremely confident. He had a way with words and could charm almost anybody. And he was, quite simply, the most handsome man I've ever seen in my entire life. Physically, he was faultless. A glorious, flowing mane of black, curly hair. Immaculate olive skin. Amazing features. Beautiful white teeth which shone as he smiled. He was tall and strong. Unsurprisingly, all the young ladies adored him! And yet, strangely, so did the men.

He seemed to be able to chat with anyone about anything, and to make those he was speaking to feel that they were 'special'. With soldiers, he would ask about their recent conflicts, showing an apparent interest in their well-being. With the priests, it was the Law. With the prophets, he would ask about Abraham, Moses or how the land was taken under Joshua. He radiated friendliness and a desire to please. Only a few of us could see through this façade. I hate to speak evil of anyone, but he was, without question, a selfish, hypocritical, lying, scheming man. He wanted only one thing: personal glory. He wanted the kingdom. And if that meant deposing and even killing his father, then that was a price he was willing to pay.

There were times when Absalom behaved as though he were already king! He had a sister called Tamar; a beautiful, faithful young woman. When one of their half-brothers treated her shamefully, he had the man killed. There were laws which dictated how the guilty party should have been dealt with, but Absalom always was a man who did things his own way. He had to flee the land for a while. He went to live with his grandparents on his mother's side, in Geshur. It didn't take him long to be accepted back into the fold. And that was when he began to make a move for the kingdom.

Each day, he would station himself outside the main gates of Jerusalem. When a man came to see the king, Absalom would ask him about the issue in question. It might have been some disagreement about an area of land, some animals, or an inheritance matter. Absalom would explain that, regrettably, the king was unable to see him – but would never fail to express his belief that the man before him was in the right.

Each day, Absalom would station himself outside the main gates of Jerusalem

"If only I was king", we used to hear him say, "I would ensure that you were treated fairly."

"If only I was king" – this was a phrase which we heard time and time again throughout the next few years. Little did any of us realise what was in the heart of this evil, grasping man.

In meetings like this, the man would invariably go to bow before Absalom. Never one to miss an opportunity, Absalom would refuse to allow this. He would hug the man in question as though he was an old and trusted friend. Time and again we saw this process repeated. Slowly but surely, Absalom managed to get almost the entire the nation on his side.

In the normal course of events, a king would have taken steps to put his rival in his place. In any other kingdom, a man who plotted to take the Crown would be dealt with extremely severely. Treason would normally carry with it the threat of imprisonment or, more likely, execution, but not on this occasion. There were, perhaps, a number of reasons for this.

Firstly, David loved Absalom – and not just because he was his son. My lord always tried to see the best in people. And he found it hard to believe that one of his own children would try to kill him and seize the throne. In addition to this, David knew that the Law of Moses would not allow any man to be killed unless he had already performed an act which demanded the death sentence. Simply planning to do something isn't the same as actually doing it.

Secondly, Absalom knew who to recruit to give him the appearance of greatness and faithfulness. If he had been alone, people would probably have ignored him after a while. But he wasn't alone. Ahithophel was often seen standing alongside him outside the walls of the city. On other occasions they arranged public meetings, with the apparent intention of strengthening the people. In truth, I knew exactly what was going on. Ahithophel had turned against David because of his treatment of Uriah and Bathsheba, and had chosen to side with his enemy.

And thirdly, David was seriously ill during this time. For many months he hardly left his bed. This was the reason why nobody was appointed to see those who came to ask questions of him. The king wasn't well enough. Even when he did get up, he looked like a little old man – ashen-faced, coughing from morning till evening, moaning with pain. His whole appearance was changed. It was almost like a form of leprosy. For a couple of years, he was a shadow of his former self.

So it came as no surprise when Absalom tried to take the kingdom. He was in Hebron when the cry went out and the trumpets sounded. Hebron – the very city from which David had reigned all those years before! At that time most of the mighty men, together with their families, had gathered at Jerusalem. This took place every few years, with the king holding a feast to express his thanks to all of the Gibbor for their support. He felt it was appropriate that the wives and children of these men were also present, as they had made sacrifices by allowing their men to remain at the palace for three months of each year.

Looking back, I can see the hand of God at work in this. Had my family been at Carmel when Absalom proclaimed himself king in Hebron, I wouldn't have known what to do. I would have been torn between a desire to serve and protect my king, and wanting to care for Naamah and the girls. Thankfully, this wasn't an issue.

By this time the king had begun to recover from the terrible illness which had afflicted him so badly over the previous few years. He was the one who made the decision to leave the city. He would not stay in Jerusalem and fight. He never wanted civil war in Israel. He gave us the choice to follow him or return home. Not one single man went back. Every one of us wanted to serve our lord – the true anointed king of Israel.

As we made our way through the gates of the city that day, none of us knew what the future held. We didn't know whether we would ever return or what we would have to face first. What we did know is that our lord was the chosen, divinely appointed ruler – and we were willing to fight for him and die for him, if necessary.

Chapter 18

The day we fled from Jerusalem

I SUPPOSE it's reasonably typical for a man to have a great deal of affection for the place where he was born, grew up, or lived for most of his life. Such a location may be despised by others, but to the individual in question it will be special. After all, Carmel was my home town and was a fantastic, beautiful, fruitful place. But the city of Jerusalem was, and always will be, different. Some may struggle to see why this should be, but for those who love Israel's God, this one key city was, and will forever be, unlike any other.

In my day it wasn't simply that Zion was a stunningly beautiful place. Or that the location was good: right there at the heart of the land, raised up high as an awesome citadel, towering over much of the surrounding area. No – what made this place truly special – unique – is that it was the city of God. I used to hear the elders call it "the city of the great King", or "God's holy hill". In symbol, the Almighty was said to live there. Of course, He is everywhere by His power. But this one key location was still portrayed as His dwelling place on earth. "He loves the gates of Zion", we were told by the prophet Nathan, more than any other city in the land. That's how wonderful it was. And now the time had come for us to leave it behind.

We could have barricaded ourselves inside the city and hoped that Absalom's rebellion would fail. But David wouldn't hear of it.

"We must leave and head to a place of safety", he told us. "In time, in God's mercy, and if it is His will, we will return. But I will not do anything which might result in this glorious city being damaged in any way. If our enemies come and spoil it, that's a matter for their consciences. I will never act in a way which might cause this holy place to be defaced."

We looked up and saw the two priests, Zadok and Abiathar coming towards us. They carried with them the ark of the covenant. I think they believed that, as David was the rightful ruler, the ark should remain in his care. Maybe they also thought that if there was a battle, the ones who possessed the ark would be more likely to win. David was adamant – the ark had to remain in the city.

"If the Almighty delights in me, He will bring me back one day, and I will be allowed to sit before His holy ark as before. But I refuse to be responsible for allowing it to be carried throughout the countryside where it might be lost, captured or damaged. This holy city is the rightful home for the ark, and it must stay here."

As we left Jerusalem behind us, a man called Ittai, together with a great number of his countrymen and their families came to meet us. They were Gittites; they had come from Gath. Strangely, they had only been with David in Zion for a few weeks. Yet they still gave every indication they wanted to come with the king.

"Ittai, you are a good and noble man", said David, "but you've only been with me for a short time. Is it fair to expect you to come with me now as I flee from this place and try to seek sanctuary somewhere else? You have been faithful and true, but it might be best if you return to Gath, at least for the time being. May God's mercy and truth rest upon you all."

I will never forget the response of that Gentile man.

"My lord, as Yahweh lives, I would rather remain with you, being chased from one place to the next, than return to Philistia. Even if it means I have to die with you, I will never leave you."

It was one of the few bright parts of what was an incredibly dark day. David hugged Ittai, and we waited while he and all the other Gittites marched to the rear of our group, ready to follow our king.

Everywhere we looked there were people crying. David had torn his clothes in sorrow and put sackcloth on his head as a sign of mourning. He removed his sandals and walked barefoot. We all did the same. We made our way down the Kidron valley and climbed up towards the Mount of Olives. I looked back and beheld the city for one last time. It seemed to glow in the early morning sun. The gates and walls which had been repaired under Joab bore testament to the importance of this one, key

David had torn his clothes in sorrow and put sackcloth on his head as a sign of mourning

location in Israel. There were tears in the eyes of every man and woman as we turned away, and began to make our way along the road that led east. It was then that a messenger arrived for David.

"Oh my lord, I come with tidings from Hebron. Absalom is king, and all the people are with him. He's planning to head to Jerusalem in the morning. And ..." he paused, as if knowing that this further piece of information would be a dagger through David's heart, "Ahithophel has chosen to make a league with him."

We all stood still, waiting to see how our lord would respond. We knew what this meant. Ahithophel was so very wise. Many of the people who may have had their doubts about Absalom would almost certainly be swayed by Ahithophel's presence. This was the very worst news that we could have received. David dropped to his knees in prayer. We all followed his example.

"Oh, my gracious Father", he pleaded, "I know that Ahithophel is a great and wise man. But please don't allow his advice to benefit those who have chosen to rebel. Turn his wise words into folly, I pray."

As we neared the summit of the Mount of Olives, we looked up and saw an elderly man coming to meet us. It was Hushai, and he had also torn his clothes and placed dirt on his head in sorrow at what was happening. This man had served David for many years, ever since the days of the Kahal. In the early years of the kingdom, like Ahithophel, he had gone throughout the nation, teaching the people, offering guidance and instruction in matters where the law wasn't understood. For the last few years he had stayed at Jerusalem as the king's special advisor. We all knew what David was thinking. This great man – courageous and faithful though he was – would only be a burden to us.

"My friend, it's good to see you", said David, "but you cannot possibly come with us. I cannot allow anyone to slow us down."

"But my lord", replied Hushai, "I want to serve and help you in any way I can. I need to assist in defeating this rebellion."

David thought for a few seconds. I know he was torn. He didn't want Hushai to be left behind, but could not guarantee his safety – or ours – if he came with us. Then he spoke up,

"Hushai, I need you to go back to the city and offer to serve Absalom. By doing this and by giving illogical advice – you may be able to undo the evil that Ahithophel has planned. You can send messages to me through the priests' sons. Please, my great friend ... as you have been loyal and faithful in the past, I need you to do the same thing now."

Every single mighty man was aware of the risk that Hushai would be taking. If he was identified as a spy, he would be executed in an instant. We all knew enough of Absalom's character to be certain of that. And trying to offer advice that would cause Ahithophel's counsel to be rejected ... surely it was an impossible task?

"My lord and my king", said Hushai, bowing low to the earth, "I will gladly do as you ask."

Oh what a man Hushai was! I offered a silent prayer, begging that he would be preserved. Much as we were about to face genuine danger and hardship, I wouldn't have traded places with him for anything.

We continued our journey. It was hard going, particularly as we had a number of women and children with us. Thankfully they were all aware of the dangers we would have faced if we had stayed too long near the city, and with God's blessing we were able to reach the village of Bahurim in good time. It was there that a relation of Saul appeared, cursing David. His name was Shimei.

"You bloodthirsty coward!" he screamed. "This is justice – justice for all the men and women from Saul's house that you've butchered. I hope Absalom's men catch you soon, you pathetic failure."

Abishai was incensed.

"How dare this man curse you, my lord? Let me go and sort him out immediately."

"You'll do no such thing, Abishai", answered the king. "And that goes for all of the mighty men. Maybe he has been sent to curse me. My own son wants me dead. Why should it surprise us if a relation of Saul feels the same way? No ... we let him curse. Maybe God will look on this and bless us for our mercy in ignoring him."

I have to admit, it wasn't easy. I knew that these accusations were completely untrue. David had done everything in his power to care for Saul's family, in keeping with the promises he had made to Saul and Jonathan. As we walked along the valley floor, Shimei followed us on the hillside above, throwing down dirt and stones, and cursing us all, calling us murderers and cowards. How I would have loved to have silenced this evil, lying man once and for all. But our lord had forbidden us, and we had to obey.

We were able to travel another three or four miles, before resting that night in a cave. It took me back to those hard days when we had fled from Saul. At that time, at least we knew that one day David would reign as king. Now it was impossible for us to know whether he would ever reclaim his throne, and whether some or all of us would die in the battles which would take place over the coming days.

Early the next day we received a message from Hushai, brought to us by the young priests:

"Get as far away as you can. Absalom is assembling all the army, and is planning to hunt you down in the morning. Keep moving. Don't delay."

We all understood the importance of this message. Every wasted minute gave our enemies an advantage. David thanked the priests for their courage, and asked them to pass on his love and gratitude to Hushai. After a short prayer, the whole company moved on.

Every member of that enormous group – every man, woman and child – was able to travel at an astonishing speed throughout that time. Looking back, it seems unlikely that such a variety of people, of all ages and abilities, should have been capable of walking such a distance in a relatively short space of time. The roads weren't good. In places they were terrible. Some of the little ones had to be carried. Others were able to walk but were so small, it seemed impossible that they would be able to keep going. But they did. Young and old – those carrying little children – those who, only a few hours previously had been unwell or even bed-ridden – were all able to keep up an amazing pace. How did they manage it? There's only one answer: the Almighty made us strong. We were blessed with a God-given degree of agility and energy, sufficient to enable us to flee the land. It had happened when Israel left Egypt, and it was happening again. And how grateful we all were for this!

As the sun began to set we reached the river Jordan. At any other time we would have been trapped. But – thanks be to God – it was almost entirely dried up. We found a ford and were able to walk across. Normally we would have needed boats to cross this mighty river. But not this time. As well as the river being so low, it was an extremely warm, clear night with not a single cloud in the sky. Thousands of stars shone above us, just as they had when I had left Carmel all those years before. The moon was as bright as I'd ever known it. We didn't even need torches to find the way across. Once again, I thanked our Heavenly Father for His goodness. I know that many others in the group did the same thing.

Finally, we arrived at the city of Mahanaim, about ten miles east of the River Jordan. It was a famous place in Israel's history. Jacob had stopped there when he returned to the land, prior to meeting with Esau. It had been given to the tribe of Gad when Israel took the land.

Ironically it had been the place where Abner had made Ishbosheth king, following Saul's death. Its name means 'double camp'. It was a tragic description of what Israel had become at this time – two separate camps of people, both with different ideals, both with different leaders.

It had been one of the saddest days in Israel's history for a long, long time. David, the rightful ruler, had been rejected in favour of his young, good-looking, smooth-talking son, who had a man of great spiritual insight at his right hand ... and the support and adoration of almost all the people. And David and his closest followers had fled the city of the Great King, seeking sanctuary beyond the Jordan.

Just when I thought it was hopeless, two astonishing things happened. Firstly, we received further information from Hushai. This news had, in fact, been reported to David only a short time after we had left the city of God. It was only relayed to the rest of the party once we were safely over the Jordan and settled in our temporary home. Ahithophel had asked for a small number of fighting men to track David down. He wanted to come after us immediately and capture only the king. It was, naturally speaking, a very logical plan. He would probably have caught us up in the plains of Jordan and, depending on the number of soldiers he had at his disposal, he may well have been successful.

But, knowing that this was extremely sensible – and that we may have been trapped by the River Jordan – Hushai had advised something else altogether. He suggested that rather than attacking immediately,

Absalom should gather the whole army of Israel together, and lead them into battle himself. And it was this advice which was accepted. When this news reached us, I and a number of the mighty men (for the first time in many days) burst into fits of laughter! Absalom, leading an army? Did he even know which end of a sword to hold? It was a chink of light – it gave us hope where previously there had been hardly any.

The second moment of encouragement came when three great men brought provisions for us. All sorts of items of food and drink, blankets and clothing were presented before David. We were amazed by their generosity. The king thanked each man personally. Their goodness was a great help at what was an extremely tragic and distressing time. I know that David never forgot these men, or the sacrifices they had made for us.

As night fell, we made ourselves and our little ones as comfortable as possible in that strange city. We all suspected that the next few weeks would bring challenges – dangers – probably even civil war in the land of Israel. But at least for the time being we, our king and our families were safe. And for this we all offered prayers of thanks to our God.

Chapter 19

Civil war in God's land

FOR THE next few weeks, we sat and we waited. We heard reports from Jerusalem from time to time. We were told that Absalom was installed as king and that he had done everything possible to stamp his authority on the nation. We had hoped that once the people had seen what he was really like, they would have turned against their new ruler. The fact that they hadn't done so was a testament to his astonishing ability to sweet-talk anyone. We heard that he had spread a tent on the top of the palace in Jerusalem and, in the sight of all the people, taken a number of David's concubines inside. We all knew what this meant. Absalom had wives already. He didn't need to touch those women who were his father's. But he was showing to everyone the utter contempt he felt for David. They all knew what he thought of Israel's former king. No matter what the outcome of this rebellion was, the relationship between father and son was surely over.

We all hoped that news might reach us that there were cracks starting to appear in the new king's administration. At the start of the fourth week, we received a lifeline. Ahithophel – who had been one of the wisest, most Godly and faithful of men – was dead. He had left Jerusalem, returned to his home city and taken his own life. We didn't know what to say. Strangely this was both good and bad news! Good, because we knew that without Ahithophel's influence, Absalom was far more likely to make mistakes – and big ones. We suspected that some of the people might refuse to follow him now that his guide was no longer by his side. But it was also bad news. Really, really bad news. Everyone was aware of the very positive influence Ahithophel had previously had on David, his mighty men, his family, his friends ... and the nation as a whole. Others were wise, but Ahithophel was wiser. Others could teach, but none like this man. He made the stories of Israel's history come to life. He could even make certain parts of the Law (which, I have to confess, I always struggled with) to sound riveting. Even though we all accepted that there was no way Ahithophel could ever have served David in the future, his death was a massive blow.

Finally, the day came for us to go out and face our foes. That last morning was a dreadful time. I'd prepared for many battles before ... too many to count, really. But this one was different. Women and children were crying. Men were unsure. Our king was still not strong enough to lead forth his mighty warriors. And the enemy soldiers were our own countrymen. I'd never known a day like it.

I still recall those final few, precious minutes with Naamah and the girls. One by one I kissed our daughters,

I still recall those final few, precious minutes with Naamah and the girls

telling them how much I loved them. The twins were only six years old. I'm not sure they realised the potential dangers which lay ahead of us. Hanniah was eight. She certainly knew what was happening. She'd always been bright. "Much more like her Mum than you", the Boss had once told me, with a smile. And he was right! She held me tighter than I'd ever known her hold me before. Although she was trying to be brave so that her younger sisters wouldn't know what was going on, she was sobbing her heart out.

"Be careful, Daddy", she begged, "and, please, please come home to us safely."

I had to fight back the tears. I didn't want her thinking I was afraid or unsure.

"Be good, my darling", I said. "Look after your Mum and the twins. I love you lots."

I gave her one last hug then looked up and saw Naamah. Oh, how I loved her! I'd loved her since the first day we'd met. Other men had a number of wives, and concubines. I never wanted anyone else.

"Take care of the girls ... and yourself", I said, as we held each other for the last time. Then the trumpet sounded, and I knew that I had to tear myself away.

"May our Father bless and keep you beneath His Almighty wings", she said, struggling to keep her emotions in check. "I'll pray for you and the others every single hour of every single day."

"Thank you, my love." There was so much that I wanted to say. So much that I felt I still had to tell her.

But there wasn't the time, and anyway I was struggling to get the words out.

"I love you, Naamah. You've always been the only one for me."

"I love you too. Always have and always will", she said, with tears streaming down her cheeks. "Now – go out there and do what you do best. And may our God bless all those who serve Him and His chosen king."

The trumpet sounded again, and we all knew it was time to go. We made our way to the open area at the front of the city and checked our weapons. All of the Gibbor were there. Every single one. We had been through so many battles before, waging war for our king and our God – but this one was unusual, for two key reasons. Firstly, we would be fighting against fellow Israelites. And secondly, we would be hopelessly and utterly outnumbered. Naturally speaking, we didn't have a hope of victory. Only with God's blessing could we win. Only if He was with us would any one of us survive the horrors that lay ahead.

David, who still looked frail but had regained some of his old sparkle, was standing on a makeshift platform raised about ten feet in the air. We all assembled before him and waited for his final instructions. He had wanted to go out with us, but we all knew that he wasn't strong enough. We explained that it would be far safer (for him and for us) if he stayed in the city. He had accepted our decision and rose to address us.

"My friends ... my loyal warriors ... courageous servants of the Most High God. These are terrible times in Israel. In days gone by, many of you have fought some immense, lengthy, bloody battles ... but always against Gentiles, against our enemies. Today, you go out against your friends, against your fellow Israelites; possibly against family members. Now, I can't tell you what to do on the battlefield. I can, of course, encourage you to be brave ... and to seek to do all in the name of our God. But if you can spare the life of a man of Israel, I would ask you please to do so. Give them the opportunity to surrender. Injure, instead of killing. We don't want to give others a reason to hate us. Now ... go forth and fight for your families, your king and your God. And may Yahweh, our loving Heavenly Father, bless and keep every one of you."

He offered a simple prayer, asking that we would be preserved, and that peace might return to God's land. When he had finished, he told us that the men of Israel were to be led by Joab and Abishai, and the Gittites, by Ittai.

Joab stood before us. He raised his sword in the air.

"Men of Israel, are you ready?"

We all shouted back that we were.

"Then let us fight like lions for King David – the true, rightful, anointed ruler of Israel."

Again, we roared our approval. David then raised his hand once more and we all stopped to listen to what he wanted to tell us. He called the three leaders – Joab, Abishai and Ittai – to stand before him.

"Please, if you capture Absalom, be gentle with him. I'm asking you, as friends ... please don't treat him roughly."

Those words were as much an instruction for us as they were for the commanders of the army. It was clear what was in the mind of our king. The mental anguish he was enduring was clear for all to see. He knew that if Absalom was at the head of the armies of Israel, he would be the first man that we would meet. And if he was killed, the rebellion would be bound to fail. In any 'normal' battle this is exactly what we would want to happen. But David had given us an express command, and we had to respect this.

We crossed the river Jordan, this time by boat, and marched silently towards the location where we had been told that the rest of the men of Israel were camped. After about eight hours we reached a massive wood in the territory of the tribe of Ephraim. We were told to wait for the enemy to come to us. There was a great deal of logic about this. We expected that there would be so many men of Israel, and so few of us, that in any 'conventional' battle – in an open plain for example – we would have been swamped. In a wood we might be able to pick them off, a few at a time. We could conceal ourselves. That was the plan anyway. Early the following day we could hear the sound of an enormous army marching. We waited for them to come, hoping, praying that we would be blessed, and that David would be returned to his rightful position as king.

When the battle began, it became clear straight away that most of those who had come against us were not soldiers at all. They were ordinary men who, just a few days before, had been working in the fields or doing other manual work. We were battle-hardened, experienced, knowledgeable warriors – and the difference showed! They walked straight into our ambushes without realising that we were waiting for them. Some didn't even have their swords drawn. Many seemed to be so terrified that fear got the better of them. Even when we were outnumbered, we still won.

On one occasion, around midday, I found myself in a clearing with two comrades, surrounded by about ten of Absalom's men. I let out a fearsome cry and lashed out at the first man. He was so unprepared that he didn't even have time to defend himself. He cried out in pain and fell to the ground, blood flowing from a gaping wound in his arm. I placed my foot on his chest, and looked up at the others.

"Now – you men have a choice", I shouted. "Surrender now, or end up like your friend here. We have no wish to kill any one of you, but we will if we have to. We fight for Israel's God and His true chosen king, David. Either throw down your weapons – or face the consequences."

Within seconds, their swords and spears clattered to the floor. I asked if any of them had any medical experience. One of them, who looked no more than about thirteen years old, said that he worked as an apprentice to a physician in Bethel.

"See to your friend, quickly", I said. "Save him if you can."

This was the pattern for many of the battles and skirmishes which took place that day. I did take the lives of Israelite soldiers over the next few hours. I can't deny that. But where possible, I gave men the chance to surrender, and most of them did just this.

But the most surprising part of the day – and the one thing which really swayed the battle in our favour – was not down to us at all. There was some kind of earthquake in the forest. Men from Absalom's army were "swallowed up". It reminded me of the account of Korah's rebellion, which Ahithophel had spoken about on many occasions. Over twenty thousand men who had followed Absalom were dead at the end of that first day. The rest had either surrendered to us or fled back to their homes. We lost fewer than a hundred soldiers.

"The battle is won, Hez", said Joab, as the sun began to set. "Victory is ours."

It was then that a young man from our army approached us.

"My lord Joab", he said, sounding a little hesitant, "I saw Absalom, hanging in a tree by his hair."

Joab laughed: "Hanging by his hair? Are you sure it was him?"

"Yes sir. No doubt about it."

"And did you kill him?" asked Joab, still apparently unable to believe what he was hearing.

"No, my lord. I know what our king commanded about his son. He wanted us to be gentle with him."

The young man led us to an enclosed place where boughs of great oak trees hung over a wide pathway. The road dipped down sharply below the trees. And there, all alone, with his hair tangled up in the branches, was

Absalom. There was no question about it. It really was him. He just hung there, his body swaying, his feet about two feet off the ground. Joab turned to the lad,

"Oh, my son! I would have given you all my worldly wealth if you had killed the captain of our enemies!"

"You could give me all the money in Israel", he replied, "and still I wouldn't kill him. I know what our Lord said. You know it as well. He told us all to be gentle with this young man. And if I had killed him and was called to stand before our king ... well, my lord ... I can hardly imagine that you would stand up and plead my cause."

"Get out of my way, boy!" snapped Joab. "I don't need any lessons in morality from you."

With that, he took a bow and three arrows and fired them expertly into the middle of Absalom's body. The rebel king let out an enormous cry of anguish and after a few seconds, his body was still.

"Cut him down", Joab commanded his men. They obeyed. Although I suspect he may already have been dead, they all began to beat him. After that they hurled his body into a ditch and threw great stones upon it. It didn't take long for the word to get around to the rest of those who had followed him. Absalom – their charming, handsome, enthusiastic new leader – was dead. The rebellion was over. Joab blew a trumpet and our men assembled before him.

"Men, we return to stand in the presence of our king. The rebels have fled. Their leader is no more. Let us give thanks to our God for His goodness today."

We bowed down and listened to the prayer offered by Abishai. But all the time I wondered what David would say or do when the news reached him that his son was dead. I suppose it had to be. There was no way he could have been permitted to live after all he had done in the last few weeks and months. But that didn't ease my concerns as to how the king would react when he heard that Joab had disobeyed his command.

News of the victory was sent to Mahanaim. Strangely, two men took the same message. An Ethiopian servant who was a superb runner was dispatched by Joab. But another man, Ahimaaz, who was the son of one of the priests, begged to be able to run as well. Initially Joab refused, but eventually he gave in and this second man was also sent out. Slowly, with our 'prisoners' bound in groups of about twenty, we made our way back to the Jordan, and then to the security of the city of the two camps. We were about half a mile from Mahanaim when Ahimaaz came out to see us.

"Our king is crying, my lord ... weeping for Absalom. He says he wishes he could have died in his place."

Now, I'd seen Joab get angry on many occasions. Sometimes over major issues. Sometimes over trivialities. But never, ever, had I seen him react to anything the way he did that day. He stormed into the city and barged into David's room. We all heard what he said. I think the whole city heard it.

"You are an embarrassment. A pathetic excuse for a king. How dare you cry, wishing that Absalom had been preserved! Maybe you'd be happy if he was still alive and we were all dead? Is that what you want? Well, is it?" I thought he was finished, but he was only just getting started.

"We have been out there, every single one of us, risking our lives to keep you and your family safe. About a hundred of our men haven't returned. And you dare to sit here, weeping like a little child? Your problem is you've forgotten where your loyalties should really lie. It seems to me that you love your enemies and hate your friends."

After a few seconds' silence, Joab began again. This time his voice was slightly softer, as though he was genuinely appealing to David to respond to his request,

"Look: the choice is yours. Either you get out there and greet those mighty men who have served you so faithfully, or – and I really mean this – there won't be one single man who will remain true to you by the end of the day. And that will be worse than anything you have had to face from the time when you were a little lad back there in Bethlehem with your few sheep, until now. Make your choice, my king. The time has come."

These were harsh words. Some of them I could agree with. Others were an exaggeration, intended to make a point. A short time afterwards, David appeared at the gate of the city, and one by one he greeted us and thanked us for our faithful service.

I made my way towards the place which had been given to my family when we first came to the city. Unsurprisingly, space was limited. We had been allocated the top of one of the houses. It wasn't much, especially after the relative luxury we had been used to back in Carmel. But at least it was home.

On the way, I looked up and saw Naamah coming to greet me. We both quickened our pace, pushing past the great numbers of other men and women. When I finally managed to reach her, we fell into each other's arms. We didn't say anything – not a single word. We just held each other. She sobbed and sobbed. All around us there were cries of joy or despair. Some men hadn't returned. But by God's grace, I had come back to my family in safety.

Mahanaim may not have been the most glorious city in Israel. There wasn't much room to spare. It wasn't particularly comfortable. And it certainly wasn't beautiful. But at that moment, in the arms of the one I loved, and knowing that the servants of the rightful King of Israel had been victorious, there was nowhere in the world I would rather have been.

Chapter 20

The return of Israel's true king

IT'S STRANGE, but sometimes we don't appreciate what we've got till it's gone. Only after something has been lost, or a situation is changed, do we realise that what we had before was worth keeping hold of, and we were wrong to let it go so easily. This is true in many aspects of life. It was most certainly true in the matter of the kingship of Israel.

For most of his time, and in the eyes of the majority of the people, David had been the ideal king – firm, but fair. He had taxed the people, but never to such an extent that they were left in poverty. And the money which was raised wasn't used solely to build his palaces, or finance a luxurious lifestyle for him, his wives and sons. It was used to benefit the kingdom as a whole: cities were built or repaired; borders were made secure. The army was strong, with men trained, equipped and ready for anything. Great tracts of desert, which previously had been barren wastelands, were irrigated and brought back to life. Industries, like fishing, were helped with money from the state. Mariners went far and wide, buying and selling. Yes, there was no question about it – with the exception of his actions with Bathsheba and Uriah – David had been a superb ruler.

He had always tried to teach and keep God's law, and had stressed the reason why it was so important. When wars had to be fought, he was almost always there at the forefront of the battle. He never asked someone to do something he wouldn't do himself. Under him, Israel had prospered in so many ways. Then another man came along, and the majority of the people were swayed, regarding David as 'yesterday's man'. But when Ahithophel took his own life, and then Absalom was killed, the people of Israel were suddenly faced with an extremely uncomfortable truth: they had rejected the best ruler they had ever had ... and now they were without a king altogether! It didn't take them long to decide what they needed to do. They would have to swallow their pride and welcome David home. Thankfully, this is precisely what the majority decided to do.

We had spent a week in Mahanaim, recovering from that weird battle, cleaning and repairing our weapons, tending to the sick and injured, and enjoying time with our families. When the call came for us to return, it was as though a dream had come true. David, as a wise and astute man, knew exactly how to act so that the people would accept him.

When the time was right for us to head back to Jerusalem, he sent a message to the elders of the tribe of Judah via the priests. He asked why they hadn't requested his return. Other tribes, it seemed, had already done so. In time they would also call for him to come home. But initially, the men of his own tribe appeared to be a little hesitant – that was until a further offer on the part of David finally swayed them.

Absalom had chosen a man called Amasa as his army commander. He was yet another of David's nephews. Knowing that he had been a popular leader amongst the men of Israel, David said that Amasa would be promoted to army commander in Joab's place. Well, it was this last comment which finally swung the people of Israel in David's favour. The leaders of Judah, especially, responded to our lord's words, almost begging for him to come home. When we made our way to the banks of the Jordan it was an extremely emotional time. Representatives of the whole nation were there – but it was the presence of the elders of Judah which moved the king most.

As we boarded the ferry boats which had been prepared to carry us over the river, I paused, listening to the cheering of the crowds. I was amazed that these people who, only a few weeks before, had wanted us all dead, were now happy to accept us as returning heroes. It seemed wrong. But I know that David was willing to forgive those who had turned against us, and he wanted us to do the same.

As the first few members of our party prepared to make their way across the river, I noticed an elderly man was standing among them. He was checking that there was enough room in each boat and helping those with little children. It was then that I remembered where I had seen him before. He was one of the three men who had met us at Mahanaim, providing food and clothing for us. His name was Barzillai. David made his way over and greeted him.

"Barzillai", he said, "I will never forget your goodness to me and my men. The entire nation had turned against us, but you remained true. This must have taken an enormous amount of courage. Had Absalom won, then you would have paid the price for your loyalty to me. You would have been executed as a traitor. I thank you once again for your kindness and love."

Barzillai was smiling as he hugged the king.

"Oh my lord, I knew you would come back. How could another man take the throne from you? You are the anointed of Yahweh, and I was certain that He would return you to your rightful place one day. I'm just glad I'm still alive to see it."

"Look, why not come with me to Jerusalem?" asked David. "I will find some quarters for you there. You can live in comfort and luxury with me in the city."

"Oh my king, I am very conscious of the honour you wish to bestow upon me", Barzillai replied, "but I don't need anything. I am content to live in my home city. I want to stay there for the rest of my days. And I want my body to be laid to rest alongside those of my parents in the family tomb. But ... if you are willing, I would ask that those blessings which you would have bestowed on me are granted to another man. My faithful servant

Chimham has been with me for many years. Are you willing for him to receive the good things you wanted to give me?"

"My friend", replied David, "I will gladly do as you ask."

As we made our way across the river, listening to the cheering of the crowds, taking in the sights, I looked up and saw one man standing at the front of the group, waiting for us to reach the river's bank. It was Shimei – the relation of Saul who had cursed us as we'd fled from Bahurim. As soon as David had crossed the river, he fell down before the king.

"Oh your majesty", he begged, "please, please forgive me. I know now how badly I acted. I should never have said all those things to you. I know that you didn't treat Saul's family badly, and I repent of what I did and said all those weeks ago. I wanted to be the very first to come to welcome you back, so that you know how sorry I am."

"How dare this miserable Benjamite even speak to you, my lord?" said Abishai. "He should be killed instantly for his actions. If you give me permission, I will ..."

"Not another word, Abishai", replied David. "No-one will die today at my hand or the hand of any of my men. I am king, and I could have him executed immediately if I wanted to. But today is a day to be joyful."

He looked down at Shimei, who was still grovelling before him.

"Get up Shimei. I won't put you to death for your sins. I give you my word."

David looked down at Shimei, who was still grovelling before him

Others also came to meet the king. One was a crippled man called Mephibosheth, Jonathan's son. David had cared for him at the palace for many years. We had all expected that he would come with us when we fled from the city, but he was nowhere to be found.

When we had journeyed from Jerusalem all those weeks before, a man called Ziba, who had served the family of Saul, had brought food and drink for us. He had told us that Mephibosheth had claimed that he was about to be made king, now that David was out of the way. I didn't know what to believe. I certainly couldn't imagine this lame man claiming the crown as his own when Absalom had rebelled. But at the time we had more pressing matters to think about – like trying to stay alive!

When Mephibosheth bowed before David, he was in a terrible state. His clothes were dirty, and his hair, beard and fingernails had grown long.

"Oh, my lord", he cried, "I know what Ziba has said about me. And it's not true. I promise you it's not true. How could I ever turn against you after all you've done for me? How could I ever believe I would be made king of this great land? I would have come with you when you fled from Jerusalem, but, as you know, I can't walk, and Ziba took all the beasts with him."

We didn't know who was lying and who was telling the truth. I suppose that it might have been possible for David to have called both men to stand before him and try to work this out, but he had enough to do already.

"Look, there's plenty of land for you and Ziba", he said to Mephibosheth, "have half each. Then whoever is telling the truth will have sufficient to live off."

"My lord and my king", replied Mephibosheth, "let him have it all. I mean it. Give him the whole estate. As long as you're back safely, that's all that matters to me."

As we made our way up from the Jordan I suspected that we would go straight to Jerusalem as quickly as possible. But we didn't. Instead David insisted that we stopped off at Gilgal. This was a city right by the river's bank. It was an extremely important location in the history of Israel. The people had stopped there when they had first entered the land after the death of Moses. It was as though our lord was acknowledging that, like Israel under Joshua, we were coming into God's land and that a new age was about to begin. Gilgal was one of the three key locations where Samuel used to teach the people. Again, it is very likely that David was thinking of that great man, and all that he had done for him in preparing him to take the throne. Now the time had come for him to retake it.

It would be nice to record that, after crossing the river and spending a short time at Gilgal, we were able to head back to the city of God, and that all the people came and welcomed David back home. Well, as I had discovered over the last few months, things rarely go as we might expect!

The tribe of Judah had come to greet David ... but the other tribes felt aggrieved about this. They even accused Judah of "stealing" David away from them! For a short time I even worried that civil war was about to break out again. Thankfully, in the mercy of the Father, this didn't happen. There were some very heated exchanges between the elders of the other tribes and those from Judah, but eventually they agreed to let things lie. I was so relieved! The thought of more warfare in the land promised to Abraham, Isaac and Jacob was almost too horrendous to contemplate.

As we neared the city of Jerusalem, I dropped to my knees in prayer and thankfulness. I wasn't the only one who did this. All around me people were praying, embracing or singing psalms to God, rejoicing that He had brought the true king of Israel home again.

When the gates of Zion loomed before us, Hushai came out to greet the king. What a man! What an astonishingly courageous, faithful, clever man! We all knew that if Absalom had seen through his pretence, he would have been executed in an instant. But with the blessing of God, he had been preserved. His "illogical" advice had been accepted and, in time, victory was ours. Later that day I sought him out and thanked him for what he had done. He was predictably humble.

"I didn't do much. It's possible that my advice to Absalom gave our king sufficient time to regroup – but it may well have happened without me."

"Oh, my lord, you're far too modest!" I replied. "You did more to ensure that our lord was successful than any warrior out on the battlefield. And for that I owe you an enormous debt of gratitude ... as does every single faithful servant of King David."

Hushai smiled.

"We all did what we could, Hez. No one man is worthy of more praise than another. We all played our parts."

"A wonderful day today", I said. "Those scenes as we neared the holy hill of Zion ... I'll never forget them as long as I live."

"Ah yes", replied Hushai, "the rightful king returning to Jerusalem in glory. It will happen again, you know, one day."

Immediately I knew what he meant. He was talking about the one whose coming had been promised, through the prophet Nathan.

"In our lifetimes?" I asked.

"No, my son, I suspect it will be one day many years from now. But the chosen ruler will definitely come. Zion will be transformed. It really will be the city of the Great King, and a place where people from all nations can come to worship and pray. What we saw today – fantastic though it was – will be nothing compared with that time of glory, when the Messiah comes to his city at last."

Again, I found myself lost in wonder at these things. I had seen so much in the service of David. I had experienced times of hardship ... and times of great glory. I had seen the chosen one return to Zion to take his place as ruler. But a greater king would come at some future stage. The promised, anointed, holy son of God will come and rule from Jerusalem, and reign over the whole earth in righteousness.

Chapter 21

Another challenge for David

WE HAD been back in Jerusalem for about two weeks when David called us all to stand before him. All the servants of the king, including the mighty men, were to be sent out from the capital to review the situation in the kingdom. How much damage had the rule of Absalom done?

Thankfully, as I arrived back in Carmel, it soon became clear that our house and fields had been virtually untouched during our absence. Some of the grain had been plundered, and a couple of sheepfolds were damaged but apart from that, everything was OK. I couldn't get too upset about this. After all, had a rebellion taken place when I was a lad, and had Nabal left his fields virtually unattended, I would really have had some fun!

I stayed in Carmel for a couple of days, making sure that Naamah and the girls were settled. I also checked on some of the older inhabitants of the city. Aunty Jemima was overjoyed to see me. As soon as I walked through the door of her house, she threw her arms around me.

"I prayed every day that you would be kept safe", she cried, wiping away tears of joy. "Thank God you're all right. We heard that the whole nation had sided with Absalom. I knew that you could only win with the blessing of the Almighty."

As I made my way back to our house, I wondered how I had been unable to appreciate her kindness and generosity to me all those years before. How could I have been so blind? I had failed to see that she had protected me from Uncle Jed when he was in one of his moods. How often had she gone hungry so that I might be fed? How many days did she spend on her hands and knees, gleaning round the corners of the fields, trying to salvage a few scraps of grain? I shuddered when I thought of how my presence in the house must have increased the everyday burdens she had to face. Thankfully, she was now in a much better place!

When I returned to Jerusalem, I knew immediately that something was wrong – seriously wrong. Everywhere I looked, men were armed, ready for battle. Others were rushing about, clearly preparing for a time of warfare. I managed to find Benaiah and asked him what was happening.

"Another rebellion has started, Hez. A Benjamite is calling all Israel to follow him. Our lord is concerned that he will cause us more trouble than Absalom. We are being sent out to try to track him down. We need to meet in the main hall when the trumpet sounds."

"What about the rest of the country?" I asked. "How many are with the enemy?"

"Almost all of Israel are with him. Those from Judah are with David. Amasa has been sent to gather all the fighting men of Judah. They should be with us by the morning."

The man who led this further revolt was called Sheba, the son of Bichri. He was from the tribe of Benjamin. Oh, those Benjamites! When would they ever accept that the royal tribe was Judah? We all knew what had been promised to the man Judah by his father Israel:

"The sceptre will not depart from Judah ..." he had been told. Judah was the tribe from which the kings would come, not Benjamin.

But ever since Saul had died, we had heard nothing but grumbling from some of the tribe of Benjamin – always whingeing about what they had lost. We saw that with Shimei, Saul's relation. How he would have loved Absalom to have won, and for David and his followers to have been wiped out! Thankfully, in the plan and purpose of God, it wasn't to be. And at least Shimei had the decency to admit that he had been wrong. But that didn't stop others from his tribe from seeking to take the throne. And Sheba, despite his reputation as a fool, was clearly able to motivate others to follow him.

I had hoped that after the hardship of the last few months – and especially as so many men from Israel had died – the people would be desperate for some peace and stability. As I made my way to my room in the city of God, I heard the trumpet sound. The time had come. We needed to fight for our lord once again. I had just enough time to retrieve my tent and a few other essentials before racing to the great hall.

Thankfully, as I arrived at the hall, I realised that I hadn't missed anything. As I looked round the room, I noticed a lot of very familiar faces. We'd been through all sorts of experiences together. We had slept in caves and dens; sometimes in the open air. We'd endured times of hunger and extreme cold. We had been hunted down by the king of the land. We'd had to fight for our lives on many, many occasions. To an outsider this may sound like an absolute nightmare! But I wouldn't have missed a second of it. Those bonds of camaraderie were special. They were unbreakable.

"Here we are again, then, Hez!"

I turned, and saw Joab. Although I could never agree with some of his actions, he was certainly loyal to David. And he was one of the greatest warriors I'd ever known – ruthless in battle; totally single-minded. I'm not sure I would have counted him as a friend. But I certainly wouldn't have wanted him as an enemy.

"Another rebellion, my lord?" I said, "and just when I thought things might get back to normal."

"That's human nature for you. This one's different though. We can't wait for him to come to us, or give him time. We must hunt him down and destroy him before he can do us any damage."

He said this in such a way that it sounded as if he was relishing the challenge. Many of us had homes and families. We had places where we would far rather have been than going into battle again. Joab lived alone, in a house in the wilderness. All that mattered to him was the army and his position as David's commander. Nothing else came close.

It was then that the king appeared with Nathan the prophet and Hushai, his special advisor. David stood up, and the room became silent.

"My faithful friends, my brothers, warriors for Israel's God. I thank you, as always, for your loyalty to me. Without your support over the last few weeks and months, my kingdom would be no more. After the last rebellion came to nothing, I longed and I prayed for stability – for peace in God's land. But it seems that we must face another enemy. And this man might cause us more hurt than my own son."

We waited for him to go on. This was a really serious situation – not only for David and for all those who were gathered before him, but for the nation of Israel as a whole.

"The man's name is Sheba, the son of Bichri. He is a Benjamite. Those who know him say that he's always been a bit of an idiot – but he clearly has sufficient authority amongst the people to lead many men in a rebellion against us. Almost all the tribes of Israel are with him. Those of Judah have indicated that they will remain true to me. I have decided that Amasa should lead the army. He knows the lords of Judah best."

I was standing next to Joab when this was announced and could sense his disapproval. He didn't say anything, but I could tell that he was far from happy. We waited for further instructions.

"Amasa was due to be here today", David explained. "I asked him to rally the forces of Judah three days ago, and we have received a report that they have gathered at the city of Gibeon. Now, if Sheba manages to get the men of the bigger cities and towns on his side, we may see the whole nation divided. We can't take that chance. And so, once again, I have to ask you to fight for me and for Israel's God. May He bless and keep you all."

After Hushai had given a brief, moving prayer, the mighty men, together with a number of faithful Gentile warriors, marched for Gibeon that night. Uncertainty filled our hearts. How many of the men of Israel would be willing to fight for Sheba? Where would the battles take place? Were the men of Judah really on David's side, or had they just said this? And how would they react if they were faced with having to kill their fellow Israelites?

As we reached Gibeon, I was pleased to see that a massive number of warriors from Judah were gathered there, with Amasa at the head. At least we wouldn't be hopelessly outnumbered this time. I began to feel a little more comfortable about things. I looked up and saw Amasa – another fine-looking, noble, courageous nephew of David. Joab went forward to greet him.

"Nice to see you, my brother", called Joab. "I hope you're well."

But then, as the two men hugged, Joab took out a short sword and stabbed his cousin in the stomach. He lifted his body off the ground, with the knife still embedded in his belly. After a few seconds Amasa fell to the floor, with blood gushing from a gaping wound. Joab, who was

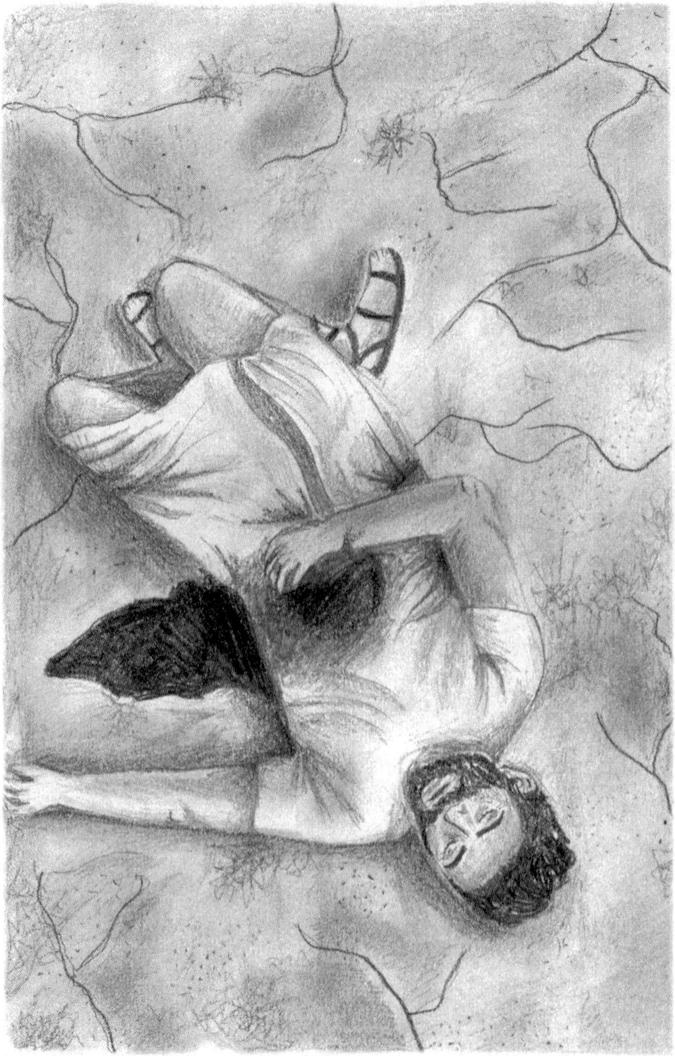

Amasa fell to the floor, with blood gushing from a gaping wound

covered in blood, walked away without a word, leaving the lifeless body of his enemy lying on the ground. Had the wound been smaller, we might have been able to stop the bleeding. We did try, but it was hopeless. By now, Joab's men were calling for the men from Judah to follow him and Abishai.

I was horrified that Joab had once again chosen to kill a man in the worst way possible. He had done this before – to Abner. Now history was repeating itself. How could a man who was so very brave on the battlefield act in a way which was so incredibly cowardly? How could he demand respect from his men when he behaved like this? I considered heading back to Jerusalem or Carmel – I was so ashamed of what had happened. But I had a job to do and, regardless of what Joab was like, I had to serve and protect my king. And that meant tracking down and killing Sheba, the enemy of the true king of Israel.

After receiving reports that our enemy had travelled up towards the Syrian border, we marched north. As we journeyed through the land, we realised that many of those who had declared their allegiance to Sheba were not really committed to the cause at all.

There were minor skirmishes on most days, but nothing more. As soon as we gave our opponents the opportunity to surrender, most of them did so without a second thought. The majority just went home. Others fell in line behind us. I wondered how far we would have to travel before we managed to find Sheba. Some said we would never be able to catch him. Others suggested that he had family in Syria. Maybe he had fled the land for good?

Finally, after around three weeks, we arrived at a city in the extreme north of the land. I'd rarely been this far north before. The place in question was called Abel-Bethmaachah, and was in the territory of the tribe of Naphtali. All the reports indicated that Sheba had sought refuge inside. It was a fine place, with sturdy walls and towers, and a massive iron gate at the front. I knew straight away that taking this place would not be easy.

"Men of Judah ... servants of the true king of the land", called Joab. "We stand here before a mighty city of Israel. As you can see, it is well fortified, and the people inside are said to have sufficient supplies to last them for many months. Now ... the enemy of our king and our God is within these walls. We cannot simply sit and wait. He may be able to send a message, calling for others to come and help him. He still has many in the land who support his claims to be ruler. So, we must build a siege-mound, enabling us to gain access to the city. Every man must help."

Over the next few days we gathered anything we could find to create that mound. The aim was to reach the top of the city walls. Others set about trying to break down part of the wall. We knew it would only be a matter of time before we were successful.

Early one morning, about a week after we had arrived, we heard a woman's voice. She was calling to Joab,

"Joab, leader of the armies of David, can you hear me?" she continued crying for about ten minutes. Finally Joab was found, and he responded to her call:

"This is Joab, commander of the armies of the true king of Israel. Why do you cry to us?"

"My lord, this city was always known as a place of learning, a place of wisdom. Now, would it be wise for you to destroy a whole city for the sake of one man? Is it fair to punish all of us for the sins of one person who has chosen to hide here? Surely that would be unjust?"

"You're right", he replied. "It would be unjust. We have no wish to shed the blood of any man or woman from this place. But a man has challenged the rightful king of the land, and we seek him so that the rebellion might be ended, and peace can return to Israel. Sheba the son of Bichri is with you. If he is killed, I give you my word that we will leave in peace."

Well, we didn't have to wait long. Within about half an hour the severed head of our enemy was thrown over the city walls. Joab blew the ram's horn, and we knew that victory was ours. After a short prayer, we began our journey back home.

Looking back, it could be argued that things had gone very well for us. The king's enemy was dead. His followers had either returned home, followed after us, or had been killed. The whole nation was aware that David would never again allow anyone to rise up and challenge him. I should have joined with those of our group who sang for joy. But I couldn't do this.

As we travelled back to Jerusalem, all I could think about was how badly Joab had behaved. I couldn't shake the feeling that he should be made to answer for his actions that day at Gibeon. This was the second time he had killed an army commander. On both occasions decent, honourable men lay dead. Both had been murdered in the same cowardly, vile way – and by a man who professed to be courageous, faithful and true.

A real mighty man would never act as Joab had. David knew it. The men of the Gibbor all knew it. And I suspect that, in his heart, even Joab knew it. He was the one appointed by David to lead, and we would never willingly disobey an order. We had always been loyal and true, seeking to follow him. But there's no way he had earned our love ... or our respect. Peace had been secured in Israel. But the hands of Joab were stained with the blood of an innocent man. And none of those who had witnessed his actions would ever forget what they had seen.

Chapter 22

Pestilence in the land ... and a holy place secured

AT LAST, it seemed that the land was at rest. No more invasions by enemy armies. No more uprisings led by disenchanted Benjamites. No more ambitious princes trying to seize the throne – just peace. Maybe I was getting old – but this was fantastic! I had reached the time when camping around besieged cities, tracking enemy soldiers for miles in the driving rain, and fighting in the open fields for hour after hour had lost a lot of its charm. I was still stationed at Jerusalem for three months each year. And I had to be willing to go out and fight for my lord at a moment's notice.

The fields in Carmel which had belonged to Nabal and Abigail were still as fruitful as ever, but they demanded a great deal of hard work. I had men working with me, of course – particularly at harvest time. But I still had the responsibility of overseeing what was planted and where, which animals to buy and breed from, and when to allow certain areas of land to lie fallow.

I remembered Abigail's kindness to those who were in need, and did my very best to maintain the high standards of generosity and goodness that had been shown by her. I tried to make gifts without anyone knowing. Items would be left at the doors of houses at night – or where grain was bought, I would deliberately give more than was actually purchased. I was determined to help anyone who was in need. But I refused to be treated unfairly.

Some of the men I employed were, quite simply, lazy. Or worse, liars. They claimed that they had worked a certain number of hours when I knew this wasn't the case. I would question this the first time – but if it happened again I would warn them that there was no way this would be allowed to continue. Most of them accepted this and changed their ways. A few needed a second warning. After that, I would politely recommend that the ones in question look for employment elsewhere! When we had reached this stage they usually got the message and never came back. I hated having to sack anyone. It was my least favourite part of the job.

Naamah and I enjoyed a long and happy marriage. That longed-for son never arrived – so I had to accept that the name "Hezrai the Carmelite" would die out after me. But our three daughters, like those born to Job were (at least in my eyes!) the most beautiful in the land. They were kind and Godly and, although we had our occasional differences, they were all that I could ever have wished for.

Naamah was, in many ways, exactly like my Mum. She never let anything get to her. Trials and tribulations came on us from time to time. There were problems with health, or issues to do with livestock or crops. But she would just accept these things and take them in her stride. When her excellent parents died within two weeks of each other, she was incredibly sad (obviously), but she believed in the promises, and knew that they would rise again. Her faith was a marvellous example to everyone she met. One of the older labourers in our fields told me that she reminded him of Abigail. I only hoped that I didn't remind him of Nabal!

One day, about ten years after Sheba's uprising had been quashed, a servant of David arrived in Carmel. He went from house to house, ending up with us. I knew the man well. He was called Hamuel, and was of the tribe of Simeon. He was good and faithful. We had chatted on many occasions in Jerusalem. He wasn't a warrior. He dealt with legal matters, such as taxation and allocation of the money which had been collected.

I was astounded when he showed me the letter which he carried with him, sealed with the king's official seal. It gave him permission to take a record of the number of fighting men in the kingdom. He seemed as surprised as I was by the request.

"Why does our lord want to know the number of warriors in the land?" I asked. "Is he anticipating another war? Are the Philistines amassing their forces near the border again?"

Hamuel shook his head, and sighed,

"No – and that's what makes this all the more surprising. There aren't any reports of enemy nations preparing for war, or of any rebellions within the nation. Since Sheba's challenge came to nothing, I think all Israel can see that David is the best man we could have as a leader."

"So why number the people? What could this possibly achieve?"

Hamuel shrugged his shoulders,

"Hez, your guess is as good as mine. Even Joab advised against this, but our lord would not be swayed."

Around the time the census was completed, I was stationed at the palace for my three-month stint. A number of the mighty men were present in the chambers of the king when the prophet Gad requested a meeting with him. We knew straightaway that something important was about to be revealed. We suspected that the king knew that he had done wrong in numbering the people and that he had confessed his sin to God in prayer.

"My lord, I have a message from Yahweh for you", advised the prophet.

"Then please, let me hear it", replied the king.

"What you did in numbering the people was wrong and judgments must be poured out upon Israel because of this. God offers you three options. There could be seven years of famine in the land, or you could flee from your enemies for three months, or there will be three days' pestilence in Israel. You must choose."

David fell to the floor, holding his head in his hands. Then he arose, very slowly, and addressed the prophet once again,

"Gad, our Heavenly Father's mercies are great. I would far rather fall into His hands than make a decision and get it wrong. Please, may the choice be made by God?"

We didn't have to wait long to see which option had been chosen. Three days of terrible pestilence descended on the entire land. A vile plague left seventy thousand men dead. It was like something out of the history books; like one of the plagues in Egypt. Some families were left entirely untouched but, even in the palace, a number lay dead. On the third day I was with the king, together with the rest of the Gibbor who were stationed at Zion. We were walking outside the palace walls. The cries of men and women rang out across the city. Many were dying. Others mourned the loss of loved ones. The whole nation seemed to be suffering.

"Oh no ... oh no!" cried David, looking up into the sky. He dropped to his knees. We all looked upwards, and then every single one of us fell to the ground, covering our eyes. A mighty angel, with a massive sword in his hand, stood over the city. It was the most terrifying thing I had ever seen in my entire life.

"It's my fault!" cried David, "it's all my fault. Please, punish me. I am the shepherd. Please, don't hurt these sheep. Take me instead."

I looked up and saw the prophet Gad, hurrying towards us. He had received a message from the Lord,

A mighty angel, with a massive sword in his hand, stood over the city

"My king, I have a commandment from our Heavenly Father for you. You must go and buy the area of land to which the angel's sword is pointing. You need to build an altar to our God there."

As you can imagine, David didn't waste any time in making his way to that part of the city! The piece of land in question was owned by a man called Ornan; he was also known as Araunah. The section which was to be bought was a raised area where he and his men threshed wheat or other crops. We called these areas "threshing floors".

Araunah was a Jebusite – but a faithful one. He had fled the city well before David had taken it, following Joab's great act of bravery in scaling the water spout. When Jebus was captured, Araunah had reclaimed the area of land which had previously belonged to his family. We all knew what a decent man he was. Very few of the other Jebusites were faithful. Araunah, like Uriah the Hittite, had learned about Israel's God and had made the decision to be associated with His people. When he saw us coming to see him, he was understandably concerned.

"My lord David", he said, bowing low before him, "What brings you to see me?"

"Araunah, I wish to buy your threshing floor to build an altar to Yahweh our God. Only when this has happened will the plague cease."

"Oh, my lord and my king", replied Araunah, "take it, please. Take it all as a gift. I don't want to be paid for this. In the presence of your mighty men and all my family, and before the only true God in heaven above, I declare this day that the threshing floor is yours. I will even give you animals for sacrifices and wood to burn. They are devoted this day, freely to you."

"Araunah", said David, "you are a good man. I thank you for your generosity. I will not forget this. But I must pay you. A sacrifice means nothing unless the one who is doing the giving actually feels it. How can I give something to God when it hasn't cost me anything? Under Moses' law, the best has to be brought. The firstfruits are God's. It's the same here. I insist that I pay you the correct amount for this site. My faith demands it of me."

Well, the price was agreed: fifty shekels of silver. David bought the threshing floor, the altar was built, and the plague came to an end. It had been a horrifying time for everyone in Israel. It seemed strange – almost wrong – that so many should die as a result of the actions of one man. Especially when he had survived the plague altogether, only having to pay out an amount of money that it might be brought to an end.

Over the next few days and weeks, many in Jerusalem – and throughout the rest of the land – pondered these events. But as life in the kingdom began to get back to normal, we soon became aware of two vital additional facts. And, slowly but surely, things began to make sense.

Firstly, we were told that it was God Himself who had moved David to number Israel. I asked the prophet Gad about this. He told me that because so many had sinned in Israel, judgments had to be poured out. The census permitted these sinners to be identified and dealt with by God. Some may call this harsh – even cruel. But as Gad explained, a potter may make a jar or dish on a wheel. If the item in question doesn't come out right – if it is made of impure clay and is hard to shape properly, then the potter starts all over again.

"We are all like the clay in God's mighty hands, Hez" explained the seer. "And if He wishes to deal with us in a particular way, He can. He is the creator. He can do what He wants with His creation."

So, why did the area of land which had been owned by Araunah have to be bought? Why was it so important? Well, in time it became clear that this was the very place where Abraham had been prepared to offer his son Isaac as a burnt offering to God. But more than that – this was the site which was to be used for an amazing temple which would be built in the days of Solomon, David's son. David had wanted to oversee the building of this "house of prayer", but he had been told that this was not possible. Much as he was disappointed by this (and we, as his faithful servants, were surprised!), we were told the reasons for this decision. David was a man of war. Throughout his life he had been a mighty warrior. The temple was to be built by a man of peace. It had to be built by Solomon.

As I sat before the prophet that day, contemplating what had gone on, I finally saw what this was all about. Sinners have to be dealt with. Our Father is so holy – so pure – that men who constantly flout His ways cannot remain untouched. By removing those who had offended Him, and ensuring that the area for the temple was obtained, the Lord God was showing the entire nation what He was demanding from His people. He was calling for the men and women of Israel to cast out the evil, Gentile practices which had crept in, and make their homes – their lives – their minds – like a holy place, giving glory to Him.

Chapter 23

David's mightiest men

ALMOST ALL rulers have people who are close to them – those they trust, those they turn to for advice or encouragement,, even correction. This was certainly the case for David. Apart from soldiers, any king needs advisors. For many years he had Ahithophel, a man with an awesome knowledge of God's word, the history of the nation, and the Law. We were all devastated when he turned against our king and sided with Absalom. We knew how hard it would be to find anyone to take his place. But life goes on. Hushai, a man of great courage and perception, stepped up and helped to fill the void which had been left. David gave Hushai the official title of "King's companion". He was at our lord's right hand, and would give him advice in vital matters relating to the security and prosperity of the kingdom.

One of David's uncles, a wise man called Jonathan, was a counsellor for the king and also the royal scribe. Another man, Jehiel, was officially appointed to oversee the king's many sons. As princes of Israel, these men all possessed a degree of wealth and authority. But David was determined that they should never abuse their positions. So this one faithful man was chosen to manage their education and training. In the case of a small number of these (Absalom especially), it could be argued that this didn't work very well – but it wasn't for want of trying! Many of David's other sons were far more like their father.

The whole government was organised to ensure that everything proceeded correctly and efficiently, with each man doing his own job, and reporting to the one above him or directly to the king.

One man was over all the treasures of the kingdom. Taxes came to him, along with any valuable items which were brought to David by traders, or donated as gifts by rulers of foreign lands. Another man was in charge of the grain stores. Others managed the king's fields, vineyards or olive groves. One man had the job of looking after David's wine supplies. There were vast cellars in Jerusalem, and he had authority over these. The king had massive numbers of sheep, goats, camels and asses: unsurprisingly, there were men nominated to take care of these animals.

And just as the civil administration of David's empire was overseen in precise detail, the entire army also followed a clearly defined pattern of organisation. Some may have regarded this as unnecessary, or even 'over the top'. But this wasn't the case at all. This specific order of all military matters ensured that everything was done correctly, and that there were always enough fighting men available at any time. Every month one man was nominated as captain, with twenty-four thousand foot soldiers at his disposal. There were twelve of these nominated leaders, and they served for the same month every year.

As well as these men, David designated one key man over each tribe of Israel. Like the rulers of the people who were chosen to spy out the land under Moses, they were the king's representatives to the men and women of their respective tribes.

The mighty men were also members of a highly organised group, with every man knowing his place. A number of these men were given positions of leadership. We knew where we stood. We were, after all, soldiers. And every army has to have a structure. There are ranks, with some having greater authority than others.

The total number of those in the Gibbor was thirty seven. David had our names carved on individual plaques made from the finest cedar wood and stained beautifully. These were hung in the room in Jerusalem where the mighty men assembled. Just to look up and see my name there was an amazing thing. It told me that I was a member of an extremely select group. We were allowed privileges that other men, even those who were high up in the army, were not able to enjoy. We had access to the king – something that the average soldier could only dream of.

So: thirty-seven key obedient, brave, fighting men – the cream of David's army. But in the room where we met, there were only thirty-six names. If ever we went out to

David had our names carved on individual plaques made from the finest cedar wood and stained beautifully

fight as a group – such as when we were dispatched to track down and kill Sheba – every man was present. But one key name was missing from the list. Whose plaque was removed? It was, in fact, Joab's. Whenever the names of the Gibbor appeared – if they were recorded in the Chronicles of the king, for example – Joab's name was absent. This was David's way of showing how shamefully he had acted when Abner and Amasa were murdered.

Which brings me to the others. It would take me too long to list all of their faithful acts! But, as we have been through so much together, I think it would be only right to record some of their most notable deeds.

There were three chief men in the group. When we went out, we would often be under the command of one of these three leaders. Their names were Adino, Eleazer and Shammah.

Adino was the mightiest man. He was the chief man in the group. In one battle alone he killed eight hundred enemy soldiers with a spear – an amazing warrior. Little wonder he was the leader and sat in the highest place when we met – normally right next to the king.

David was with Eleazar and a number of young soldiers one day in a battle with the Philistines. Maybe because they were outnumbered – or maybe because the Philistines were related to Goliath and were very tall – the men of Israel turned and ran away. That left Eleazar and David there alone. Well, they refused to run! They backed themselves into a corner and fought for the rest of the day. Eleazer killed so many Philistines that his hand stuck to the handle of his sword. Only after the enemy had been routed did the Israelite soldiers return to take some of the spoils.

Shammah achieved fame in a similar situation. Lots of Philistine warriors were gathered together in an area where lentils were growing. Again, the men of Israel fled. And again, Shammah refused to do so. He stayed there for the whole of the day, defending that patch of land. But when he returned and stood before David, he was quick to acknowledge that it was God who had blessed him, enabling him to achieve his great victory.

One day, during the reign of Saul, David and these three mighty men were in the cave of Adullam. The whole of the Philistine army was spread out in Rephaim, the Valley of the Giants. An enormous number of enemy soldiers were stationed there, all of them armed and ready for war. They had taken certain Israelite towns and cities. And one of these was Bethlehem! David's home city was in Gentile hands and Saul couldn't (or wouldn't) do anything about it.

"Oh, how I wish I could have a drink of water from the well in Bethlehem", said David.

Looking back, I think it's very clear what he was asking for. It wasn't that the water from the well in Bethlehem was any better than the water from the wells in Israel! No – he just longed that Bethlehem might be free, and that he could sit at the side of the well in safety, as he had when he was young.

Whether the three mightiest men misunderstood what he meant, I don't really know. But they clearly decided that David's wish for a drink of water from the well at Bethlehem should be granted. They managed to break through the Philistines' defences, reached the well, and drew some water out. They then carried it to David and presented it to him. Much as he was extremely impressed by the bravery of these men – and I imagine he would have loved to drink that water – he would not. He poured it out as an offering to the Lord, saying that had he drunk it, it would have been like drinking the blood of the men who had risked their lives for him.

After these first three, who were over the whole number of the Gibbor, there were a further three great warriors. They were 'second-in-command' among the mighty men. Their exploits were also legendary – but the first three exceeded them. And this is where the absence of Joab's name is notable. Of the 'second three', only two names were ever recorded. Abishai, Joab's brother, was one of this group. So too was Benaiah. But the third name was absent. It was something we never spoke about – but we all knew what had happened. David had removed Joab's plaque for his sinfulness in killing two other army commanders.

What a tragedy! Joab could have – and should have – been so much more than he was. Yes, he was probably the most fearsome warrior I've ever fought alongside. If I could choose anyone to fight for my life, he would be the one. But if I needed someone to give me guidance from God's word, I would choose almost any other man. Killing on the battlefield is one thing. Murdering fellow Israelites in cold blood because you feel they have insulted your family, or are a threat to your position, is another thing altogether. Yet Joab never showed even the slightest hint of remorse for what he had done. A mighty man in one sense. But a complete and utter coward in another.

Abishai was the "unofficial" captain of this second group of three leaders. In one battle, he killed three hundred enemy men with a spear.

The second leader of this group of three was also an amazing individual, Benaiah the son of Jehoiada. Those who remembered his father told us that he was just like him – totally focused, immensely brave and with a spirituality which was, sadly, often lacking amongst other mighty warriors. He was from a town called Kabzeel, way down in the south of the land, near the border with Edom.

Benaiah was younger than many of us in the group – but in every way he was a senior man in terms of faith and valour. He was the leader of two different groups known as the Cherethites and Pelethites. Many of these were Gentiles – yet more faithful Philistines – who had come to David and embraced Israel's hope. They had very specific jobs. The Cherethites were executioners. Their job was to hunt down and kill. This was the duty of all of the mighty men from time to time. But this one group was singled out by the king for this specific task, and when called upon to act, they were ruthlessly efficient. The Pelethites were official couriers. They were trained to run to deliver important messages. If army reinforcements were needed, then a number of these men would be sent to call for back-up. They would fight as well, of course, but their primary duty was to take the king's words, or those of Joab, to the rest of the nation. They always performed this task superbly.

Benaiah fought great and mighty enemies on many occasions. One day he killed two men of Moab, who were like lions. They were notorious for their savagery – but they met their match the day they strayed into Israelite territory and Benaiah was patrolling that particular part of the border. Despite being outnumbered, this mighty man was victorious.

On another occasion he came up against an Egyptian giant – not quite as tall as Goliath. This man was "only" seven-and-a-half feet tall! He still towered over us. He carried a gigantic spear and, perhaps unusually for a battlefield warrior, was also extremely handsome. But all these attributes counted for nothing when this faithful Israelite went out to meet him, armed with nothing but a staff. In the duel that followed, Benaiah grabbed the Egyptian's spear and plucked it from his grasp. He then killed this enemy of Israel with his own spear!

One day, Benaiah and three other men had been caught in a snowstorm on the way back to the Kahal. Suddenly, one of the other men slipped into a pit which had been dug by some locals to trap wild animals. The trap had worked very well: a mountain lion was in there! Without a thought for his own safety, Benaiah leapt into the pit, and with just his trusty staff, he killed the lion. The other man, who had been seriously injured, was lifted out. The reports of this astonishing incident spread through the camp like wildfire. The elders were certainly impressed, likening it to resurrection.

Finally on the list – although not because he was least in importance – is Uriah the Hittite. I can't find words to do this man justice. He may not have been born an Israelite, but he was a son of Abraham in his heart. Oh, how tragic that he should have died as he did. But how wonderful that the mercy of God should be poured out so freely on those who had sinned! And how fitting that Bathsheba, far from being cast off for her actions, became the wife of David through whom the royal line would continue. Solomon was her son, and he sat on the throne in Jerusalem after his father's death.

Of the other men who aren't listed above, all I can say is that they were the best friends a man could ever wish for – brave, trustworthy and loving. They were chosen out of all the men of Israel to serve and protect the king and (with the exception of Joab) not one of them ever let him down. Being called to be one of this group of men was an honour of which, at the time, I didn't really think I was worthy. Even to this day I still struggle with it. Why did David choose me? All I know is that I never took the blessings of the group for granted or betrayed any of my colleagues. They would have died for me, and I know in my heart that I would have laid down my life for any one of them.

One day, as I sat in Jerusalem, looking out over the Hinnom valley towards Bethlehem, Hushai joined me. We had both witnessed so many amazing events in the service of our king. Hushai had been with us in the days of the Kahal, then at Ziklag and Hebron. And, of course, he had played a massive role in bringing the rebellion of Absalom to an end. He was no warrior, but he was a mighty man, nonetheless – one of the mightiest of all.

"The men of the Gibbor are great and noble warriors, Hez", he said. "I know our king is very grateful to you all for your loyalty and courage. Without your support he may never have regained his kingdom."

"My lord, Hushai", I answered, "it's an honour to serve. It always has been. And for as long as I am permitted to be part of this group, it always will be."

"You know, after our day there will be other groups of mighty ones."

"When the Messiah comes?" I asked.

"Well, I believe that there will always be mighty men and women. In days gone by there were some who served our Heavenly Father. In the days of Noah, Abraham and even the Judges there were a few faithful individuals, who worshipped the only true God. And I'm sure that after our day, there will be others who will continue to maintain the standards that our king has impressed upon us. They will believe the promises which have been made to the fathers of this great nation, and to our lord, David. There will always be a remnant – a small number of people who are, like the men of the Gibbor, mighty. They may not necessarily fight as you have done Hez, but they will be mighty all the same."

I gazed out at the Judean countryside, amazed by the beauty of the scenery before me. The sun was beginning to set, and the greens and browns of the fields contrasted superbly with the blood-red sky. It would be a fine day tomorrow!

"And what about when the Messiah is here?" I asked. "Will the men of the Gibbor be together again?"

"Ah, yes", replied Hushai, "but in that day, a greater number of mightier people will be gathered before David's son, all of them immortal; made like the angels of heaven. And what a day that will be! It will be the start of something truly wonderful. A time of rebirth, not only for Jerusalem or the land of Israel, but for the whole world. God has things in store for His chosen people that will be better than anything that this life has to offer. And by grace, they will be granted to all who seek to serve Him faithfully."

Chapter 24

Standing before my king for the final time

BY THE time I was sixty years old, I was beginning to suffer physically. I had experienced so many nights out in the cold – either in my teenage years, with David in the Kahal, or on the battlefield – and now I was starting to pay the price. My joints ached like mad, and I found that marching great distances was something I was unable to do any more. Fighting in the army required so much more than just courage – physical fitness and agility were essential. A man had to be able to wield a sword or spear for hours on end. I had reached the stage where, sadly, I knew that this was beyond me.

Thankfully, I wasn't alone in feeling this way. Others – including the king himself – were also slowing down. Occasionally, soldiers refused to accept that they had to back off from active service. They had to be made to retire. But normally a man would know and accept it without a word of complaint. It had to be. No one can continue doing what we had done for ever. It was time to allow others to step in and take our place.

One day, a week after my sixty-third birthday and during one of my stays at Jerusalem, I was called to stand before the king. Even kneeling before him was hard. By now David was an elderly man. He hadn't been out of the palace for many months. He felt the cold really badly. Although he was still focused on the kingdom, and specifically on preparations for the building of the great temple at Jerusalem, he was well aware that his days on the throne in Zion were numbered. Solomon, his son, would soon reign in his place.

"Hez, you have served faithfully for many, many years", he said, with a smile. "Now, come and sit with me for a while."

"My lord", I replied, taking the seat beside him, "I wouldn't have missed any part of it. You were always a fair and faithful master. And the friendship of the Kahal – and then of the Gibbor – these things were too glorious for words. Do you remember when we first met?"

He thought for a few seconds.

"Ah yes. Just outside the city of Hebron, wasn't it?"

"That's right, on the Beersheba road. I had managed to get myself into debt, gambling, and the crook who had taken all my money had caught up with me. A few seconds later and I would have been dead."

"That's what we call providence", he replied. "The angels of Almighty God were sent to guide me to you. I could have been anywhere in the land ... but I just happened to be there. What did you think of the Kahal when you first joined us? Be honest with me."

"My lord, it was like the family I had lost. It was wonderful – absolutely wonderful. I found friendship, encouragement and love. But most importantly, I found those who were willing to teach me about Yahweh, the Mighty One of Abraham, Isaac and Jacob ... and the Hope of Israel. I had been a dead man. Then in the Kahal, under your guidance, I came alive."

We chatted for a while about those times that we had shared together. We talked about Saul and Jonathan. There were tears in David's eyes as he spoke of his great friend, of the love they had shared, and how his life had been taken. We spoke of our days in Ziklag and then in Hebron. And we talked about taking Jebus and transforming it into the city of God.

"I made some terrible mistakes in my time as king, Hez. I think you know how sorry I was, and still am, for the hurt I caused. But the message came from our Father through Nathan: my sin was put away. And for that I was then, and always will be, immensely grateful. The tough times which followed those days – when my own son seized the throne – they were some of the hardest parts of my entire life. But the mighty men stayed true to me when almost everyone else had turned away. They were always there for me. You, Hez ... you were always there for me. Thank you, my friend, thank you."

He rose from his seat and hugged me. We remained in that embrace for a couple of minutes. Not a word was spoken, but we both knew what this was all about. This was to be our last meeting – at least in this life. And as the king was unable to go out before the armies of Israel

David rose from his seat and hugged me

any more, so the time had come for me to lay down my sword and spear.

"My lord and my king", I said, "I believe it is time for another to take my place in the Gibbor. With your permission, I will clear my possessions from my room later today, and head back to Carmel in the morning."

"I understand, Hez. It comes to us all. Sarah was given strength by the Father, so that she could bear a son when she was ninety. Moses was sustained by God so that when he was a hundred-and-twenty years old he was still as strong as he had been in his youth. The same was true for Caleb – able to fight giants at Hebron when he was aged eighty-five. But that's not the way it is today. Mortality, Hez. We all have to slow down eventually."

For a few minutes, we sat in silence. There didn't seem to be much left to say. I've never been that good with words, and anyway, all sorts of feelings were welling up inside me. I would have struggled to express myself adequately. We rose from our seats, and David placed his hands on my shoulders. I gazed into the eyes of Israel's great king. He was an elderly man, but those eyes still held their old gleam.

"Hez, you are now, and will always be, one of my mightiest men. May our God bless you and keep you. Goodbye, my friend."

"Thank you, my lord. May God's blessing rest upon you and on your seed. May the promised Messiah soon come." I was determined not to let my emotions get the better of me, but there were tears in my eyes, as there were in David's, as we said our final farewells.

"Goodbye my king, and thank you once again for your friendship and love ... thank you for everything."

I went to the room in the palace where the mighty men assembled. A few of the Gibbor were there, and I told them about my meeting with David and my decision to 'retire'. They all understood. Although there were plenty of words of encouragement and thanks for what I had done, not one of them tried to persuade me to act differently. Perhaps that told me all I needed to know!

I then made my way back to my room and gathered up my things. The next morning I ate a simple meal alone and was on the road as soon as the sun was up. I didn't want to see David or any of the Gibbor that day. Somehow, it wouldn't have seemed right. It was time for me to leave Jerusalem behind – at least for a while.

As I arrived back in Carmel, I reflected on the last few hours – and indeed, on these last forty years in the service of that great man. Without David's influence, my life would have been empty, worthless, hopeless. He and his men had shown me what had been missing. They taught me about the Hope of Israel; about the promised seed; about the Kingdom of God which will come one day. Oh how blessed I was that I had been allowed to share in these things!

In Carmel, Naamah was waiting for me, her face a picture of love and goodness. Her life hadn't always been easy. With a husband who was away for at least three months of every year, she often had to play the role of father and mother to our three wonderful daughters, as well as managing the estate which had been left to us by

Abigail. No one could have done a better job. She was a fantastic wife and a fantastic mother. When I was down – after the death of Uriah, or when we lost our son – she was the one who would encourage me, help me, care for me, forgive me.

Carmel had been a barren, empty, desolate place for me in my teenage years. But later it had become everything I could have wished for – and so, so much more. "Fruitful"? Most certainly. Thanks to the influence of others in my life – Aunty Jem, the Boss, Han, David, Uriah, Naamah and our daughters – my life had definitely been one of fruitfulness. Most especially it was thanks to the blessings of our gracious, loving Heavenly Father. Without His mercy and goodness, my entire existence would have been pointless.

I am aware that I don't have many years left ahead of me. But I also know that the promises speak of a resurrection and the greatest of all gifts: immortality, and incorruptibility, for God's chosen ones. And I know that when that time comes, a massive number of mighty men (and women) will glorify Him, transforming the whole world, under the guidance of David's greater son. Each night I pray that I will be numbered amongst that group of people, when the Messiah comes to reign from God's holy hill of Zion ... when the Gibbor of Israel stand in the earth once again.

List of key characters

Abiathar. One of the priests who assisted David by feeding information to him during his exile. *(2 Samuel 15:24-29)*

Abigail. Nabal's wife. Appealed to David for mercy. Married to David following her husband's death. *(1 Samuel 25:23-42)*

Abishai. Joab's brother. One of the mighty men. *(1 Samuel 26:6; 2 Samuel 23:18)*

Abner. Saul's uncle and army commander. *(1 Samuel 14:50)*

Absalom. David's son. Grandson of the King of Geshur. Good-looking and charming. Turned against his father and seized the throne. *(2 Samuel 3:3; 14:25; 15:1-10)*

Achish. King of Gath, with whom David lived for a time. *(1 Samuel 27:2)*

Ahimaaz. The son of one of the priests, through whom messages were passed to David during Absalom's rebellion. *(2 Samuel 15:27)*

Ahithophel. David's counsellor. One of the wisest of men. Formerly loyal to David; afterwards united with Absalom. The grandfather of Bathsheba. *(2 Samuel 16:23; 15:31; 23:34; 11:3)*

Amasa. Absalom's army commander. David's nephew. *(2 Samuel 17:25)*

Araunah. A Jebusite, also known as Ornan, who owned an area of land in Jerusalem which David was commanded to buy. *(2 Samuel 24:16-25; 1 Chronicles 21:15)*

Asahel. Joab and Abishai's brother. One of David's mighty men. Known for his ability as a runner. *(2 Samuel 3:30; 2:18)*

Barzillai. One of three men who aided David and his men when they fled from Jerusalem. *(2 Samuel 17:27)*

Bathsheba. Wife of David. Formerly the wife of Uriah the Hittite. Mother of Solomon. *(2 Samuel 11:3,26,27; 12:24)*

David. Youngest son of Jesse. Former shepherd who was anointed as king of Israel in place of Saul. Killed Goliath, the giant from Gath. King over Judah and then the whole of Israel. A man "after God's own heart". *(1 Samuel 16:11-13; 17:49-51; 2 Samuel 2:4; 5:3; Acts 13:22)*

Gad. Seer who guided David. *(1 Samuel 22:5)*

Hezrai (Hez). A Carmelite. One of David's mighty men. Our "author". *(2 Samuel 23:35)*

Hushai. David's "friend" / counsellor. This appears to have been an official position in the administration of David and Solomon. He remained loyal to David throughout his life. Played a major role in defeating Absalom's rebellion. *(2 Samuel 15:32-37; 17:7-15; 1 Chronicles 27:33)*

Ishbosheth. Saul's son, made king by Abner after his father's death. *(2 Samuel 2:8-10)*

Ittai. A Gentile (from Gath), who remained loyal to David when Absalom rebelled. *(2 Samuel 15:19-22)*

Joab. David's nephew, the son of Zeruiah, David's sister. Gained access to Jebus (Jerusalem). The commander of David's army. *(1 Chronicles 2:15,16; 11:6; 18:15)*

Jonathan. Saul's son. Accepted that he would not reign after his father, and that David was to take his place. *(1 Samuel 23:17)*

Jonathan (2). The son of one of the priests, through whom messages were passed to David during Absalom's rebellion. *(2 Samuel 15:27)*

Mephibosheth. Jonathan's lame son, cared for by David before the rebellion of Absalom. *(2 Samuel 9:6,11)*

Nabal. A landowner in Carmel. Married to Abigail. Refused to assist David. *(1 Samuel 25)*

Nathan. Prophet through whom God's words were revealed to David. *(2 Samuel 7,12)*

Obed-edom. A Gittite. The Ark was stored at his house following a failed attempt to bring it to Jerusalem. He was blessed by God during this time. *(2 Samuel 6:10,11)*

Samuel. Israel's seer and guide in the days before the mortal monarchy. Anointed Saul and David. *(1 Samuel 3:19–4:1; 10:1; 16:13)*

Saul. A Benjamite. The first human king of Israel. Faithful at first, but wayward later. *(1 Samuel 10:1,24; 11:15; 15:11)*

Sheba. A Benjamite who tried to take the kingdom after Absalom's rebellion had failed. Initially, most of the nation followed him. Died at Abel of Bethmaachah. *(2 Samuel 20:1,2,22)*

Shimei. A relation of Saul who accused David of murdering Saul and his family. *(2 Samuel 16:5-8)*

Solomon. David and Bathsheba's son. The one chosen by God to reign after David. *(1 Kings 1:13; 1 Chronicles 28:5)*

Uriah. One of David's mighty men. A Hittite by birth. Married to Bathsheba. *(2 Samuel 23:39; 11:3)*

Zadok. One of the priests, who assisted David by feeding information to him during his exile. *(2 Samuel 15:24-29)*

Zeruiah. David's sister. Mother of Joab, Abishai and Asahel. *(1 Chronicles 2:15,16)*

Part of David's family tree

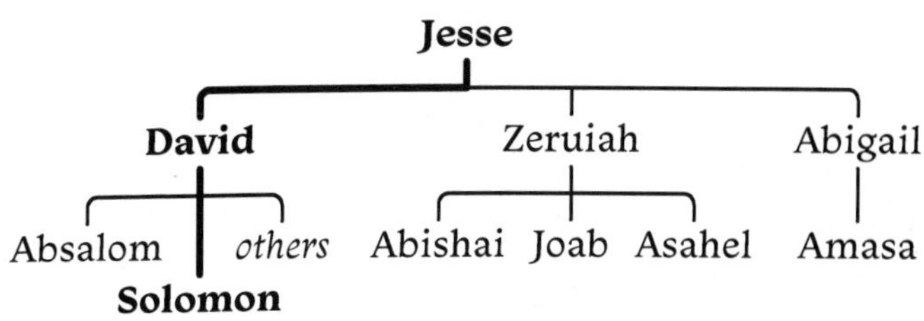

List of scriptural references

Chapter 1

- A firstborn son was normally named after his father. *(Luke 1:59)*
- Saul enlisted men of Israel into the army. *(1 Samuel 8:11,12)*
- Orphans were usually cared for by family members. *(Esther 2:7)*

Chapter 2

- Nabal was a wealthy landowner in Carmel. *(1 Samuel 25:2)*
- He was a fool. *(1 Samuel 25:3,25)*
- Abigail, Nabal's wife, was beautiful and spiritually-minded. *(1 Samuel 25:3)*
- Saul set up a monument in Carmel. *(1 Samuel 15:12)*

Chapter 3

- Nibshan, on the shore of the Dead Sea, was near "the City of Salt". *(Joshua 15:62)*
- Hebron existed as a city in Abraham's day. He built an altar to the Lord there. *(Genesis 13:18)*

- The tomb of Abraham and his family was in Hebron. *(Genesis 23:19; 49:31)*
- Sepulchres were often painted white in Bible times. *(Matthew 23:27)*
- Caleb had taken the city of Hebron, having defeated the giants who lived there previously. *(Joshua 14:12,13; 15:14; Judges 1:10,20)*
- Hebron was a priestly city, and a city of refuge. *(Joshua 21:13)*
- Jebus was also known as Salem, Ariel, Zion and Jerusalem. *(Psalm 76:2; Isaiah 29:1; 2 Samuel 5:7; Judges 19:10)*
- David was known and respected by the people of Israel, and it was accepted by many that he would reign after Saul. *(2 Samuel 5:2)*

Chapter 4

- (Unsurprisingly) there were men who would deceive and rob others in Bible times! *(Proverbs 6:12-14)*

Chapter 5

- Part of the watchman's job was to keep the gates of the city. *(Psalm 127:1)*

Chapter 6

- David was a mighty man well before his elevation to the throne. *(1 Samuel 16:18)*
- David and his men lived in camps before he became king. *(1 Samuel 23:22-24)*
- "Kahal" is a Hebrew word, meaning an assembly. *(Exodus 12:6)*
- It is the Old Testament equivalent of the New Testament word "ecclesia". *(Psalm 22:22; Hebrews 2:12)*

- "Harps" were played in David's day. *(1 Samuel 16:16,23)*
- David was a shepherd to those who served him. *(2 Samuel 24:17)*
- Some of those who followed David had been in debt. *(1 Samuel 22:2)*
- David was originally of Bethlehem. *(1 Samuel 17:15)*
- He had worked as a shepherd, and had killed lions and bears, protecting his father's flock. *(1 Samuel 17:34)*
- Samuel had anointed David in the presence of his brothers. *(1 Samuel 16:13)*
- David had played the harp before Saul. *(1 Samuel 16:16,23)*
- He had killed Goliath, the Philistine champion. *(1 Samuel 17:49-51)*
- He acknowledged that it was God who gave him the victory. *(1 Samuel 17:37,47)*
- Saul sent bands of soldiers to try to capture David. *(1 Samuel 19:20)*
- Jonathan was a man of great faith. *(1 Samuel 14:6)*

Chapter 7

- Of those who followed David, many were in distress, in debt, or discontented. *(1 Samuel 22:2)*
- For many years there were hardly any swords in Israel. *(1 Samuel 13:19-22)*
- David and some of his men went to Nob, where they were given food and the sword of Goliath by the priests. *(1 Samuel 21:1-6,8,9)*
- They saw Doeg the Edomite there. *(1 Samuel 21:7)*
- "Great men are not always wise." *(Job 32:9)*

Chapter 8

- Asahel was known for his ability as a runner. *(2 Samuel 2:18)*
- Samuel and David had laid down detailed plans for the organisation of the nation. *(1 Chronicles 9:22)*
- Gentiles can be beneficiaries of the promises to Abraham. *(Genesis 12:3; Galatians 3:8)*
- Sin and death will finally be no more when the world is transformed. *(1 Corinthians 15:26)*
- Those blessed with immortality will be made like the angels. *(Luke 20:36)*
- They will glorify God on the earth. *(Revelation 5:10; 22:3)*
- The Lord Jesus (the Messiah) is the promised seed. *(Galatians 3:16)*
- He died, but was raised to life again. *(Acts 4:10)*
- The faithful are like the dust of the earth, stars in the sky, and sand by the sea shore. *(Genesis 13:16; 15:5; 22:17)*

Chapter 9

- Ahithophel was a great man, with an awesome knowledge of the ways of God. *(2 Samuel 16:23)*
- David fled to Gath because of Saul's pursuit of him. *(1 Samuel 21:10)*
- Jesse was an old man when David was anointed king; he and David's mother were sent to live in Moab for a time. *(1 Samuel 17:12; 22:3,4)*
- The number of men with David had risen to more than four hundred by this stage. *(1 Samuel 22:2)*
- A number of mighty men (Hebrew, "Gibbor") were with David. *(2 Samuel 10:7)*
- The prophet Gad journeyed with David, giving him advice and instructions from God. *(1 Samuel 22:5)*

- Saul oversaw the murder of eighty-five priests at Nob. His men refused to be involved in this; Doeg the Edomite obeyed Saul's command. One man (Abiathar) escaped, and came to David, remaining with him. *(1 Samuel 22:9-23)*
- David went to the city of Keilah and rescued those who had been taken captive by the Philistines. *(1 Samuel 23:1-5)*
- David was told that the men of Keilah would betray him to Saul, and relocated to the wilderness of Ziph. *(1 Samuel 23:12-14)*
- Jonathan came to David, and strengthened him. *(1 Samuel 23:16-18)*
- The men of Ziph betrayed David to Saul, and he fled to Hachilah, then to Maon. He was on one side of a mountain, with Saul and his men on the other, when Saul heard that the Philistines had invaded, and he had to call off the hunt. *(1 Samuel 23:19-28)*
- David relocated to Engedi. *(1 Samuel 23:29)*
- David and some of his men hid in a cave; Saul entered. David cut off the corner of his robe, then regretted it. *(1 Samuel 24:1-8)*
- David made the king aware that he had spared his life. Saul promised not to chase David any more. David agreed to protect Saul's family. *(1 Samuel 24:8-22)*

Chapter 10

- Samuel's death. *(1 Samuel 25:1)*
- Nabal was a wealthy man in Carmel. *(1 Samuel 25:2,3)*
- David's men had protected Nabal's fields and animals. *(1 Samuel 25:15,16,21)*
- Nabal refused to give any assistance to David, at which point David determined to kill all the males in Nabal's house. *(1 Samuel 25:5-13,22)*

- Four hundred men went with David; two hundred guarded the camp. *(1 Samuel 25:13)*
- Abigail appealed for mercy. David accepted her words. *(1 Samuel 25:24-35)*
- Nabal died; Abigail married David. *(1 Samuel 25:37-42)*

Chapter 11

- David and his men returned to Ziph (Hachilah); they were betrayed to Saul by the Ziphites for a second time. *(1 Samuel 26:1-3)*
- David went down to Saul's camp; all the men were asleep. *(1 Samuel 26:5-7)*
- The Urim and Thummim were in the breastplate of the High Priest. They were used to give an answer to certain key questions. *(Exodus 28:30; Numbers 27:21; 1 Samuel 28:6)*
- A deep sleep from God came upon Adam when Eve was created. *(Genesis 2:21-23)*
- David and Abishai went to the place where Saul was lying. David refused to kill him. His spear and cruse of water were removed. *(1 Samuel 26:6-12)*
- David called to Saul, telling him that he had spared his life. Saul promised never to pursue him again. The two items were returned. *(1 Samuel 26:13-25)*
- David and those with him went to live in Gath. *(1 Samuel 27:1-3)*
- Saul decided not to pursue David. *(1 Samuel 27:4)*
- David was given Ziklag by the King of Gath. *(1 Samuel 27:5-7)*

Chapter 12

- Tirzah and Jerusalem were beautiful places in Old Testament times. *(Song of Solomon 6:4)*

- David and his men went out from Ziklag and defeated various Gentile groups. *(1 Samuel 27:8-12)*
- Achish, King of Gath, believed that David had turned against the Israelites. *(1 Samuel 27:12–28:2)*
- David appeared to be willing to fight against Israel; some Philistines were unhappy about this, and he was not permitted to go out with them. *(1 Samuel 29)*
- When they returned to Ziklag, they found that a band of Amalekites had destroyed the city, and taken many hostages. *(1 Samuel 30:1-5)*
- Some spoke of stoning David. *(1 Samuel 30:6)*
- David "encouraged himself in the LORD his God". *(1 Samuel 30:6)*
- Six hundred men marched with David to recover those who had been taken. Some were too tired to complete the journey. *(1 Samuel 30:9,10)*
- They found an Egyptian, who had been a slave of the Amalekites. He was ill and had been left to die. He asked David to promise that he would not be delivered to his master, then led him to the Amalekites' camp. *(1 Samuel 30:11-15)*
- The Amalekites were spread out over a large area, with spoil from many cities in Judah and from the Philistines. *(1 Samuel 30:16)*
- The attack began at twilight, and lasted until the evening of the next day. All were killed, except 400 who escaped on camels. Every captive was recovered alive. A great amount of spoil was taken. *(1 Samuel 30:17-20)*
- David made a list of thirteen key areas / cities in Israel from which spoils may have been taken, or where he had been aided in previous years. He sent the spoils to these places. *(1 Samuel 30:26-31)*

Chapter 13

- An Amalekite arrived at Ziklag with items belonging to Saul. He said that Saul and his sons were dead. He claimed to have found Saul, mortally wounded, and to have ended his life. *(2 Samuel 1:1-10)*
- David and his men mourned and fasted for the rest of the day. *(2 Samuel 1:11,12)*
- The Amalekite expected to receive a reward from David, but was executed at David's command. *(2 Samuel 4:10; 1:13-16)*
- David mourned for Saul and especially for Jonathan. *(2 Samuel 1:17-27)*
- David was instructed by God to go to Hebron. He and his men travelled there from Ziklag. *(2 Samuel 2:1-3)*
- Men from Judah came to David, acknowledging him as the rightful king. David was anointed. *(2 Samuel 2:4)*
- David commended the men of Jabesh for their actions in recovering the bodies of Saul and his sons. *(2 Samuel 2:5-7)*
- Abner made Ishbosheth, Saul's son, king over the rest of the land. *(2 Samuel 2:8-10)*
- During a battle between the men that followed David and those who were loyal to Ishbosheth, Asahel, brother of Joab, was killed by Abner. *(2 Samuel 2:12-32)*
- Ishbosheth accused Abner of a sin he hadn't committed. Abner switched allegiances to David. *(2 Samuel 3:7-12)*
- David requested that his wife, Michal, be returned to him. *(2 Samuel 3:13)*
- Abner persuaded the rest of Israel to follow David. *(2 Samuel 3:17-19)*
- Abner came to Hebron, and made a league with David. *(2 Samuel 3:20,21)*
- After Abner had departed, Joab called him back and murdered him. *(2 Samuel 3:22-27)*

- David was grieved at this. He followed the funeral procession of Abner, mourning. *(2 Samuel 3:28-39)*
- Ishbosheth was murdered by two of his servants. They beheaded him, and brought the severed head to David. David had these men killed for this act. *(2 Samuel 4)*

Chapter 14

- Representatives of the rest of Israel came to David, acknowledging him as the rightful king. He was anointed again. *(2 Samuel 5:1-3)*
- His first act as king was to take Jebus. The Jebusites taunted him, claiming the city was impregnable. *(2 Samuel 5:6)*
- David promised that whoever climbed the gutter and gained access to the city would be his army commander. Joab did this. *(2 Samuel 5:8; 1 Chronicles 11:6)*
- Jebus (Jerusalem) was rebuilt / repaired. Joab was instrumental in this. *(2 Samuel 5:9; 1 Chronicles 11:8)*
- The Philistines gathered, ready for war. Israel won the battle, and the enemies' idols were burned. *(2 Samuel 5:17-21)*
- The Philistines gathered again. David was told not to attack until he heard the sound of marching in the trees. Another immense victory for Israel followed. *(2 Samuel 5:22-25)*
- The ark was brought to Jerusalem. It had been at the home of a man called Obed-edom, a Gittite, following a previous (failed) attempt to bring it to Zion, when Uzzah was killed. *(2 Samuel 6:1-11)*
- David brought the ark to Zion. He wore a linen ephod. Much rejoicing! *(2 Samuel 6:12-19)*

Chapter 15

- David wanted to build a house for the Lord. He was told by Nathan that he would not be permitted to do this. *(2 Samuel 7:1-9)*
- Promises were made to him. These relate to David, his family, Israel and, most importantly, David's seed (descendant) who would also be the Messiah and the son of God – Jesus Christ. *(2 Samuel 7:10-16; Luke 1:32)*

Chapter 16

- Ahithophel was extremely wise, speaking God's words. *(2 Samuel 16:23)*
- All sins may be summarised as: "the lust of the flesh, and the lust of the eyes, and the pride of life." *(1 John 2:16)*
- Forgiveness is granted when there is repentance and confession of sins. *(Proverbs 28:13)*
- Various battles were fought against Gentile nations in the early years of David's reign, with great success. *(2 Samuel 8:1-14)*
- David had attempted to show kindness to the new King of Ammon, following his father's death. This was misunderstood, and David's servants were treated shamefully. *(2 Samuel 10:1-5)*
- Battles followed, with the Ammonites being allied with others (Syrians). Israel was successful. *(2 Samuel 10:6-19)*
- With the war against Ammon still continuing, David remained at Jerusalem. He looked upon Uriah's wife, Bathsheba, and committed adultery. *(2 Samuel 11:1-4)*
- She sent a message to David, telling him she was pregnant. *(2 Samuel 11:5)*
- David called Uriah to Jerusalem. After he refused to return to his home, he was sent back to the battle. *(2 Samuel 11:6-14)*

- Uriah died in battle. This had been arranged by Joab, at the express instruction of David. *(2 Samuel 11:15-17)*
- The punishment for adultery under the Law of Moses was death for both parties. *(Leviticus 20:10)*
- Bathsheba married David, and she bore him a son. *(2 Samuel 11:27)*

Chapter 17

- The son born to David and Bathsheba died, aged seven days. *(2 Samuel 12:18)*
- The Law of Moses demanded death by stoning for those guilty of adultery. *(Leviticus 20:10)*
- David was made aware of his sin through the prophet Nathan. *(2 Samuel 12:1-12)*
- He confessed his sin, and it was "put away". *(2 Samuel 12:13)*
- David and Bathsheba were blessed with other sons. One of them, Solomon, became a man of great faith. *(2 Samuel 12:24)*
- David had many other sons. *(1 Chronicles 3:1-9)*
- Absalom was a son of David. His mother was the daughter of the King of Geshur. He was extremely good-looking and able to charm almost anyone. *(2 Samuel 3:3; 14:25; 15:6)*
- Absalom arranged the murder of his half-brother, Amnon, for his mistreatment of his sister, Tamar. *(2 Samuel 13:1-36)*
- After this, Absalom fled to Geshur. In time, he was allowed to return. *(2 Samuel 13:37–14:33)*
- He stood outside of the city and talk to men who wanted to see the king. He did this for two years, and was able to get the whole of the nation on his side. *(2 Samuel 15:1-7)*
- David loved Absalom. *(2 Samuel 13:39; 14:1)*
- Ahithophel sided with Absalom. *(2 Samuel 15:12,31)*

- David was (almost certainly) seriously ill at this time. *(Psalm 38:5-11; 41:8)*
- Absalom proclaimed himself king at Hebron. *(2 Samuel 15:7-12)*
- The mighty men fled from Jerusalem with David. *(2 Samuel 16:6)*

Chapter 18

- Jerusalem was known as the "city of the great King" and God's "holy hill of Zion". *(Psalm 48:2; 2:6)*
- The gates of Zion are loved by the Lord more than any other place in Israel. *(Psalm 87:2)*
- Zadok and Abiathar brought the ark out, intending to take it with them. David refused to allow it to leave the city. *(2 Samuel 15:24-29)*
- Ittai the Gittite followed David with six hundred men from Gath. *(2 Samuel 15:18-22)*
- News reached David that Ahithophel had sided with Absalom. He prayed that his advice might not benefit Absalom. *(2 Samuel 15:31)*
- Hushai wanted to come with David. He was persuaded to remain at Jerusalem and pretend to act as an advisor to Absalom, in an effort to defeat Ahithophel's advice. *(2 Samuel 15:32-37)*
- Shimei, a relation of Saul, cursed David. David refused to punish him. *(2 Samuel 16:5-13)*
- David received a message from Hushai, advising him to get far away from the city, as quickly as possible. *(2 Samuel 17:16)*
- The people of Israel were made strong at the time of the Exodus. *(Psalm 105:37)*

- David and those with him reached the city of Mahanaim. *(2 Samuel 17:24)*
- Ahithophel had wanted to take a number of soldiers and attack David. Hushai, seeking to defeat Ahithophel's advice, had suggested gathering the whole army together, and that these men should be led by Absalom. This advice was accepted. *(2 Samuel 17:1-14)*
- Three men brought provisions for David and those with him. *(2 Samuel 17:27-29)*

Chapter 19

- Absalom had taken David's ten concubines who had been left in Jerusalem. *(2 Samuel 16:20-22)*
- Ahithophel took his own life when his advice was refused. *(2 Samuel 17:23)*
- David was not permitted to go out to battle because of weakness. *(2 Samuel 18:2,3)*
- David's army was led by three men: Joab, Abishai and Ittai. *(2 Samuel 18:2)*
- He asked them to deal gently with Absalom. This request was heard by all David's fighting men. *(2 Samuel 18:5)*
- The battle took place in the wood of Ephraim. *(2 Samuel 18:6)*
- David's men were victorious. Twenty thousand of Israel died. *(2 Samuel 18:7)*
- "The wood devoured more ... than the sword." *(2 Samuel 18:8)*
- Absalom was trapped by his hair in an oak. One soldier told Joab, who said he should have killed him, and would have been rewarded. This man quoted David's words to Joab. *(2 Samuel 18:9-13)*

- Joab fired three arrows into Absalom's heart. His body was cut down, beaten, and thrown into a ditch. *(2 Samuel 18:14-17)*
- Two men carried the news to David. One of these was a Cushite (called "Cushi" in the KJV); the other was Ahimaaz, the son of Zadok the priest. *(2 Samuel 18:19-33)*
- David grieved for Absalom. Joab reprimanded him. David composed himself and greeted his men upon their return from the battle. *(2 Samuel 19:1-8)*
- People used the tops of houses and sometimes even lived on them. *(Proverbs 21:9)*

Chapter 20

- The people of Israel requested that David return to rule over them. David reprimanded the tribe of Judah for not calling for his return first. *(2 Samuel 19:9-11)*
- David promised that Amasa, who had been Absalom's army commander, would replace Joab. *(2 Samuel 17:25; 19:13)*
- Barzillai was offered the chance to come to Jerusalem. He declined, and his servant Chimham took his place. *(2 Samuel 19:31-40)*
- Shimei came to David, begging for mercy. David promised he would not be killed. *(2 Samuel 19:16-23)*
- Mephibosheth came to welcome David. A discussion followed as to why he hadn't gone with David when he fled from the city. *(2 Samuel 19:24-30)*
- The majority of the people argued with the tribe of Judah, claiming that David had been "stolen" from them. *(2 Samuel 19:41-43)*

Chapter 21

- Sheba, a 'worthless' man, tried to take the throne from David. Many from Israel followed him. *(2 Samuel 20:1,2)*
- "The sceptre shall not depart from Judah ..." *(Genesis 49:10)*
- Joab was buried in his own house in the wilderness. *(1 Kings 2:34)*
- David had called for Amasa to assemble the fighting men of Judah. This took longer than expected. He gathered them at Gibeon. *(2 Samuel 20:4,5,8)*
- David was aware of the danger he would face if Sheba was able to take refuge in one of the major cities. *(2 Samuel 20:6)*
- All the mighty men, and others, went out after Sheba. *(2 Samuel 20:7)*
- Joab murdered Amasa. *(2 Samuel 20:8-10)*
- David's men journeyed north, eventually tracking Sheba down to a city called Abel of Bethmaachah. *(2 Samuel 20:14)*
- They besieged the city, and attempted to break down the walls. *(2 Samuel 20:15)*
- A wise woman spoke with Joab, and arranged for Sheba to be executed, and his head to be thrown over the city wall. *(2 Samuel 20:16-22)*

Chapter 22

- Job had three daughters, who were the most beautiful in the land. *(Job 42:13-15)*
- The Lord was angry with Israel, and He moved David to number them. *(2 Samuel 24:1,2)*
- Joab advised against this. *(2 Samuel 24:3)*
- David acknowledged his sin, and was offered three options by God, through the prophet Gad. He asked for this choice to be left with the Father. *(2 Samuel 24:10-14)*

- Three days of pestilence followed. Seventy thousand died. *(2 Samuel 24:15)*
- A mighty angel appeared at the threshing floor of Araunah the Jebusite, with a sword in his hand, about to destroy Jerusalem. He was stopped by God. *(2 Samuel 24:16)*
- David pleaded that he should suffer, not the people. He was told to buy the threshing floor, and build an altar there. *(2 Samuel 24:17,18)*
- Araunah offered the area of land free to David. The king refused, and insisted on paying the correct price. *(2 Samuel 24:19-25)*
- The land in question was the same location as the place used for Abraham's symbolic sacrifice of Isaac. It would later be the site of the temple under Solomon. *(Genesis 22:2; 2 Chronicles 3:1)*

Chapter 23

- David's servants and mighty men:
- Hushai, David's "friend" / companion. *(2 Samuel 15:37; 1 Chronicles 27:33)*
- Jonathan, David's uncle. His counsellor and scribe. *(1 Chronicles 27:32)*
- Jehiel: over the king's sons. *(1 Chronicles 27:32)*
- Men were appointed to oversee the king's treasures, storehouses, fields, vineyards, wine cellars, fruit trees, and animals. *(1 Chronicles 27:25-31)*
- Rulers ("princes") of each tribe were nominated. *(1 Chronicles 27:16-22)*
- A man was chosen each month of the year as captain over twenty-four thousand fighting men. *(1 Chronicles 27:1-15)*
- There were thirty-seven key mighty men. *(2 Samuel 23:39)*

- Only thirty-six are actually named, which may imply that Joab's name had been removed from the list because of his sin. *(2 Samuel 23:8-39)*
- Adino, Eleazer and Shammah were the "first three". They performed many mighty acts, including fetching water for David from the well of Bethlehem while the Philistines had control of the city. *(2 Samuel 23:8-17)*
- Abishai, Joab's brother, was one of the "second three". *(2 Samuel 23:18,19)*
- Benaiah was also one of these "second three". He killed two lion-like men of Moab, an Egyptian giant, and a lion in a pit on a snowy day. The last one of this second trio is unnamed (possibly Joab – see above). *(2 Samuel 23:20-22)*
- Hezrai the Carmelite: our 'author'. *(2 Samuel 23:35)*
- Uriah the Hittite. Bathsheba's husband. *(2 Samuel 23:39)*

Chapter 24

- David felt the cold late in life. *(1 Kings 1:1)*
- He made preparations for the temple which would be built under Solomon. *(1 Chronicles 22)*
- Sarah was ninety when she bore Isaac. *(Genesis 17:17)*
- Moses was as strong at one hundred and twenty as he had been when he was a young man. *(Deuteronomy 34:7)*
- Caleb was as strong at eighty-five as he had been when he was forty. *(Joshua 14:10,11)*
- David's greater son will reign from Jerusalem one day. *(Psalm 2; 72)*